To myself alone could I look

1 3 5 7 9 10 8 6 4 2

Vintage
20 Vauxhall Bridge Road,
London SW1V 2SA

Vintage Classics is part of the Penguin Random House
group of companies whose addresses can be found at
global.penguinrandomhouse.com

Penguin
Random House
UK

Jane Eyre was first published in 1847 and *Villette* was first published in 1853

This short edition published by Vintage in 2020

penguin.co.uk/vintage

A CIP catalogue record for this book is available from the British Library

ISBN 9781784876050

Typeset in 10.5/14.5 pt FreightText Pro
by Jouve (UK), Milton Keynes
Printed and bound in Great Britain by Clays Ltd, Elcograf S.p.A.

Penguin Random House is committed to a sustainable future for our
business, our readers and our planet. This book is made from Forest
Stewardship Council® certified paper.

MIX
Paper from
responsible sources
FSC
www.fsc.org
FSC® C018179

Independence

CHARLOTTE BRONTË

VINTAGE MINIS

Contents

1

Casting Off

ON QUITTING BRETTON, which I did a few weeks after Paulina's departure – little thinking then I was never again to visit it: never more to tread its calm old streets – I betook myself home, having been absent six months. It will be conjectured that I was of course glad to return to the bosom of my kindred. Well! the amiable conjecture does no harm, and may therefore be safely left uncontradicted. Far from saying nay, indeed, I will permit the reader to picture me, for the next eight years, as a bark slumbering through halcyon weather, in a harbour still as glass – the steersman stretched on the little deck, his face up to heaven, his eyes closed: buried, if you will, in a long prayer. A great many women and girls are supposed to pass their lives something in that fashion; why not I with the rest?

Picture me then idle, basking, plump, and happy,

stretched on a cushioned deck, warmed with constant sunshine, rocked by breezes indolently soft. However, it cannot be concealed that, in that case, I must some-how have fallen over-board, or that there must have been wreck at last. I too well remember a time – a long time, of cold, of danger, of contention. To this hour, when I have the nightmare, it repeats the rush and saltness of briny waves in my throat, and their icy pressure on my lungs. I even know there was a storm, and that not of one hour nor one day. For many days and nights neither sun nor stars appeared; we cast with our own hands the tackling out of the ship; a heavy tempest lay on us; all hope that we should be saved was taken away. In fine, the ship was lost, the crew perished.

As far as I recollect, I complained to no one about these troubles. Indeed, to whom could I complain? Of Mrs Bretton I had long lost sight. Impediments, raised by others, had, years ago, come in the way of our intercourse, and cut it off. Besides, time had brought changes for her too: the handsome property of which she was left guardian for her son, and which had been chiefly invested in some joint-stock under-taking, had melted, it was said, to a fraction of its original amount. Graham, I learned from incidental rumours, had adopted a profession; both he and his mother were gone from Bretton, and were understood to be now in London. Thus, there remained no possibility of dependence on others; to myself alone could I look. I know not that I was of a self-reliant or active nature; but self-reliance and exertion were forced upon me by circumstances, as they are upon thousands besides; and when Miss Marchmont, a maiden lady of our neighbourhood, sent for me, I obeyed her behest, in the hope that she might assign me some task I could undertake.

Miss Marchmont was a woman of fortune, and lived in a handsome residence; but she was a rheumatic cripple, impotent, foot and hand, and had been so for twenty years. She always sat up-stairs: her drawing-room adjoined her bed-room. I had often heard of Miss Marchmont, and of her peculiarities (she had the character of being very eccentric), but till now had never seen her. I found her a furrowed, gray-haired woman, grave with solitude, stern with long affliction, irritable also, and perhaps exacting. It seemed that a maid, or rather companion, who had waited on her for some years, was about to be married; and she, hearing of my bereaved lot, had sent for me, with the idea that I might supply this person's place. She made the proposal to me after tea, as she and I sat alone by her fireside.

'It will not be an easy life,' said she candidly, 'for I require a good deal of attention, and you will be much confined; yet, perhaps, contrasted with the existence you have lately led, it may appear tolerable.'

I reflected. Of course it ought to appear tolerable,

I argued inwardly; but somehow, by some strange fatality, it would not. To live here, in this close room, the watcher of suffering, sometimes, perhaps, the butt of temper, through all that was to come of my youth; while all that was gone had passed, to say the least, not blissfully! my heart sunk one moment, then it revived; for though I forced myself to *realize* evils, I think I was too prosaic to *idealize*, and consequently to exaggerate them.

'My doubt is whether I should have strength for the undertaking,' I observed.

'This is my own scruple,' said she; 'for you look a worn-out creature.'

So I did. I saw myself in the glass, in my mourning-dress, a faded, hollow-eyed vision. Yet I thought little of the wan spectacle. The blight, I believed, was chiefly external: I still felt life at life's sources.

'What else have you in view – anything?'

'Nothing clear as yet: but I may find something.'

'So you imagine: perhaps you are right. Try your own method, then; and if it does not succeed, test mine. The chance I have offered shall be left open to you for three months.'

This was kind. I told her so, and expressed my gratitude. While I was speaking, a paroxysm of pain came on. I ministered to her; made the necessary applications, according to her directions, and, by the time she was relieved, a sort of intimacy was already formed between us. I, for my part, had learned from the manner in which she bore this attack, that she was a firm, patient woman (patient under physical pain, though sometimes perhaps excitable under long mental canker); and she, from the good-will with which I succoured her, discovered that she could influence my sympathies (such as they were). She sent for me the next day; for five or six successive days she claimed my company. Closer acquaintance, while it developed both faults and eccentricities, opened, at the same time, a view of a character I could respect. Stern and even morose as she sometimes was, I could wait on her and sit beside her with that calm which always blesses us when we are sensible that our manners, presence, contact, please and soothe the persons we serve. Even when she scolded me – which she did, now and then, very tartly – it was in such a way as did not humiliate, and left no sting; it was rather like an irascible mother rating her daughter, than a harsh mistress lecturing a dependent: lecture, indeed, she could not, though she could occasionally storm. Moreover, a vein of reason ever ran through her passion: she was logical even when fierce. Ere long a growing sense of attachment began to present the thought of staying with her as companion in quite a new light; in another week I had agreed to remain.

Two hot, close rooms thus became my world; and

a crippled old woman, my mistress, my friend, my all. Her service was my duty – her pain, my suffering – her relief, my hope – her anger, my punishment – her regard, my reward. I forgot that there were fields, woods, rivers, seas, an ever-changing sky outside the steam-dimmed lattice of this sick-chamber; I was almost content to forget it. All within me became narrowed to my lot. Tame and still by habit, disciplined by destiny, I demanded no walks in the fresh air; my appetite needed no more than the tiny messes served for the invalid. In addition she gave me the originality of her character to study: the steadiness of her virtues, I will add, the power of her passions, to admire, the truth of her feelings to trust. All these things she had, and for these things I clung to her.

For these things I would have crawled on with her for twenty years, if for twenty years longer her life of endurance had been protracted. But another decree was written. It seemed I must be stimulated into action. I must be goaded, driven, stung, forced to energy. My little morsel of human affection, which I prized as if it were a solid pearl, must melt in my fingers and slip thence like a dissolving hailstone. My small adopted duty must be snatched from my easily contented conscience. I had wanted to compromise with Fate: to escape occasional great agonies by submitting to a whole life of privation and small pains.

Fate would not so be pacified; nor would Providence sanction this shrinking sloth and cowardly indolence.

One February night – I remember it well – there came a voice near Miss Marchmont's house, heard by every inmate, but translated, perhaps, only by one. After a calm winter, storms were ushering in the spring. I had put Miss Marchmont to bed; I sat at the fireside sewing. The wind was wailing at the windows: it had wailed all day; but, as night deepened, it took a new tone – an accent keen, piercing, almost articulate to the ear; a plaint, piteous and disconsolate to the nerves, trilled in every gust.

'Oh, hush! hush!' I said in my disturbed mind, dropping my work, and making a vain effort to stop my ears against that subtle, searching cry. I had heard that very voice ere this, and compulsory observation had forced on me a theory as to what it boded. Three times in the course of my life, events had taught me that these strange accents in the storm – this restless, hopeless cry – denote a coming state of the atmosphere unpropitious to life. Epidemic diseases, I believed, were often heralded by a gasping, sobbing, tormented, long-lamenting east wind. Hence, I inferred, arose the legend of the Banshee. I fancied, too, I had noticed – but was not philosopher enough to know whether there was any connection between the circumstances – that we often at the same time hear of disturbed volcanic action in distant parts of the world; or rivers suddenly rushing above their banks; and of strange high tides flowing furiously in on low sea-coasts. 'Our globe,' I had said to myself, 'seems at such periods torn and disordered; the feeble amongst us wither in her distempered breath, rushing hot from steaming volcanoes.'

I listened, and trembled; Miss Marchmont slept.

About midnight, the storm in one half hour fell to a dead calm. The fire, which had been burning dead, glowed up vividly. I felt the air change, and become keen. Raising blind and curtain, I looked out, and saw in the stars the keen sparkle of a sharp frost.

Turning away, the object that met my eyes was Miss Marchmont awake, lifting her head from the pillow, and regarding me with unusual earnestness.

'Is it a fine night?' she asked.

I replied in the affirmative.

'I thought so,' she said; 'for I feel so strong, so well. Raise me. I feel young to-night,' she continued; 'young, light-hearted, and happy. What if my complaint be about to take a turn, and I am yet destined to enjoy health? It would be a miracle!'

'And these are not the days of miracles,' I thought to myself, and wondered to hear her talk so. She went on directing her conversation to the past, and seeming to recall its incidents, scenes, and personages with singular vividness.

'I love Memory to-night,' she said: 'I prize her as my

best friend. She is just now giving me a deep delight; she is bringing back to my heart, in warm and beautiful life, realities – not mere empty ideas – but what were once realities, and that I long have thought decayed, dissolved, mixed in with grave-mould. I possess just now the hours, the thoughts, the hopes of my youth. I renew the love of my life – its only love – almost its only affection; for I am not a particularly good woman: I am not amiable. Yet I have had my feelings, strong and concentrated; and these feelings had their object; which, in its single self, was dear to me, as, to the majority of men and women, are all the unnumbered points on which they dissipate their regard. While I loved, and while I was loved, what an existence I enjoyed! What a glorious year I can recall – how bright it comes back to me! What a living spring – what a warm, glad summer – what soft moonlight, silvering the autumn evenings – what strength of hope under the ice-bound waters and frost-hoar fields of that year's winter! Through that year my heart lived with Frank's heart. O my noble Frank – my faithful Frank – my *good* Frank! so much better than myself – his standard in all things so much higher! This I can now see and say – if few women have suffered as I did in his loss, few have enjoyed what I did in his love. It was a far better kind of love than common; I had no doubts about it or him: it was such a love as honoured, protected, and elevated, no less than it gladdened her to whom it was given. Let me now ask, just at this moment, when my mind is so strangely clear, – let me reflect why it was taken from me? For what crime was I condemned, after twelve months of bliss, to undergo thirty years of sorrow?'

'I do not know,' she continued, after a pause: 'I cannot – *cannot* see the reason; yet at this hour I can say with sincerity, what I never tried to say before – Inscrutable God, Thy will be done! And at this moment I can believe that death will restore me to Frank. I never believed it till now.'

'He is dead, then?' I inquired in a low voice.

'My dear girl,' she said, 'one happy Christmas Eve I dressed and decorated myself, expecting my lover, very soon to be my husband, would come that night to visit me. I sat down to wait. Once more I see that moment – I see the snow-twilight stealing through the window over which the curtain was not dropped, for I designed to watch him ride up the white walk; I see and feel the soft firelight warming me, playing on my silk dress, and fitfully showing me my own young figure in a glass. I see the moon of a calm winter night, float full, clear and cold, over the inky mass of shrubbery, and the silvered turf of my grounds. I wait, with some impatience in my pulse, but no doubt in my breast. The flames had died in the fire, but it was a bright mass yet; the moon was mounting high, but she was still visible from the lattice; the clock neared ten; he rarely tarried later than this, but once or twice he had been delayed so long.

'Would he for once fail me? No – not even for once; and now he was coming – and coming fast – to atone for lost time. "Frank! you furious rider," I said inwardly, listening gladly, yet anxiously, to his approaching gallop, "you shall be rebuked for this: I will tell you it is *my* neck you are putting in peril; for whatever is yours is, in a dearer and tenderer sense, mine." There he was: I saw him; but I think tears were in my eyes my sight was so confused. I saw the horse; I heard it stamp – I saw at least a mass; I heard a clamour. *Was* it a horse? or what heavy, dragging thing was it, crossing, strangely dark, the lawn? How could I name that thing in the moonlight before me? or how could I utter the feeling which rose in my soul?

'I could only run out. A great animal – truly, Frank's black horse – stood trembling, panting, snorting before the door; a man held it: Frank, as I thought.

'"What is the matter?" I demanded. Thomas, my own servant, answered by saying sharply, "Go into the house, madam." And then calling to another servant, who came hurrying from the kitchen as if summoned by some instinct, "Ruth, take missis into the house directly." But I was kneeling down in the snow beside something that lay there – something that I had seen dragged along the ground – something that sighed, that groaned on my breast, as I lifted and drew it to me. He was not dead; he was not quite unconscious. I had him carried in; I refused to be ordered about and thrust from him. I was quite collected enough, not only to be my own mistress, but the mistress of others. They had begun by trying to treat me like a child, as they always do with people struck by God's hand; but I gave place to none except the surgeon; and when he had done what he could, I took my dying Frank to myself. He had strength to fold me in his arms; he had power to speak my name; he heard me as I prayed over him very softly; he felt me as I tenderly and fondly comforted him.

'"Maria," he said, "I am dying in Paradise." He spent his last breath in faithful words for me. When the dawn of Christmas morning broke, my Frank was with God.

'And that,' she went on, 'happened thirty years ago. I have suffered since. I doubt if I have made the best use of all my calamities. Soft, amiable natures they would have refined to saintliness; of strong, evil spirits they would have made demons; as for me, I have only been a woe-struck and selfish woman.'

'You have done much good,' I said; for she was noted for her liberal almsgiving.

'I have not withheld money, you mean, where it could assuage affliction. What of that? It cost me no effort or pang to give. But I think from this day I am about to enter a better frame of mind, to prepare myself for reunion with Frank. You see I still think of Frank more than of God; and unless it be counted that in thus loving the creature so much, so long, and so exclusively, I have not at least blasphemed the Creator, small is my chance of salvation. What do you think, Lucy, of these things? Be my chaplain and tell me.'

This question I could not answer: I had no words. It seemed as if she thought I *had* answered it.

'Very right, my child. We should acknowledge God merciful, but not always for us comprehensible. We should accept our own lot whatever it be, and try to render happy that of others. Should we not? Well, to-morrow I will begin by trying to make you happy. I will endeavour to do something for you, Lucy: something that will benefit you when I am dead. My head aches now with talking too much; still I am happy. Go to bed. The clock strikes two. How late you sit up; or rather how late I, in my selfishness, keep you up. But go now; have no more anxiety for me: I feel I shall rest well.'

She composed herself as if to slumber. I, too, retired to my crib in a closet within her room. The night passed in quietness; quietly her doom must at last have come: peacefully and painlessly: in the morning she was found without life, nearly cold but all calm and undisturbed. Her previous excitement of spirits and change of mood had been the prelude of a fit; one stroke sufficed to sever the thread of an existence so long fretted by affliction.

2

Turning a New Leaf

MY MISTRESS BEING dead, and I once more alone, I had to look out for a new place. About this time I might be a little – a very little, shaken in nerves. I grant I was not looking well, but on the contrary, thin, haggard, and hollow-eyed; like a sitter-up at night, like an overwrought servant, or a placeless person in debt. In debt, however, I was not; nor quite poor; for though Miss Marchmont had not had time to benefit me, as, on that last night, she said she intended, yet after the funeral, my wages were duly paid by her second cousin, the heir, an avaricious-looking man, with pinched nose and narrow temples, who, indeed, I heard long afterwards, turned out a thorough miser: a direct contrast to his generous kinswoman, and a foil to her memory, blessed to this day by the poor and needy. The possessor, then, of fifteen pounds; of health though worn not broken, and of a spirit in similar condition; I might still, in comparison with many people, be regarded as occupying an enviable position. An embarrassing one it was, however, at the same time; as I felt with some acuteness on a certain day, of which the corresponding one in the next week was to see my departure from my present abode, while with another I was not provided.

In this dilemma I went, as a last and sole resource, to see and consult an old servant of our family; once my nurse, now housekeeper at a grand mansion not far from Miss Marchmont's. I spent some hours with her; she comforted, but knew not how to advise me. Still all inward darkness, I left her about twilight; a walk of two miles lay before me; it was a clear, frosty night. In spite of my solitude, my poverty, and my perplexity, my heart, nourished and nerved with the vigour of a youth that had not yet counted twenty-three summers, beat light and not feebly. Not feebly, I am sure, or I should have trembled in that lonely walk, which lay through still fields, and passed neither village nor farm-house, nor cottage; I should have quailed in the absence of moonlight, for it was by the leading of stars only I traced the dim path; I should have quailed still more in the unwonted presence of that which to-night shone in the north, a moving mystery – the Aurora Borealis. But this solemn stranger influenced me otherwise than through my fears. Some new power it seemed to bring. I drew in energy with the keen, low breeze that blew on its path. A bold thought was sent to my mind; my mind was made strong to receive it.

'Leave this wilderness,' it was said to me, 'and go out hence.'

'Where?' was the query.

I had not very far to look: gazing from this country parish in the flat, rich middle of England – I mentally saw within reach what I had never yet beheld with my bodily eyes; I saw London.

The next day I returned to the hall, and asking once more to see the housekeeper, I communicated to her my plan.

Mrs Barrett was a grave, judicious woman, though she knew little more of the world than myself; but grave and judicious as she was, she did not charge me with being out of my senses: and, indeed, I had a staid manner of my own which ere now had been as good to me as cloak and hood of hodden gray; since under its favour I had been enabled to achieve with impunity, and even approbation, deeds that if attempted with an excited and unsettled air, would in some minds have stamped me as a dreamer and zealot.

The housekeeper was slowly propounding some difficulties, while she prepared orange-rind for marmalade, when a child ran past the window and came bounding into the room. It was a pretty child, and as

it danced, laughing, up to me – for we were not stran-
gers (nor, indeed, was its mother – a young married
daughter of the house – a stranger) – I took it on my
knee. Different as were our social positions now, this
child's mother and I had been schoolfellows, when I
was a girl of ten and she a young lady of sixteen; and
I remembered her – good-looking, but dull – in a
lower class than mine.

I was admiring the boy's handsome dark eyes,
when the mother, young Mrs Leigh, entered. What a
beautiful and kind-looking woman was the good-
natured and comely, but unintellectual girl become!
Wifehood and maternity had changed her thus, and
I have since seen them change others even less
promising than she. Me she had forgotten. I was
changed too; though not, I fear, for the better. I made
no attempt to recall myself to her memory: why
should I? She came for her son to accompany her in
a walk, and behind her followed a nurse carrying an
infant. I only mention the incident because, in
addressing the nurse, Mrs Leigh spoke French (very
bad French, by the way, and with an incorrigibly bad
accent, again forcibly reminding me of our school-
days); and I found the woman was a foreigner. The
little boy chattered volubly in French too. When the
whole party were withdrawn, Mrs Barrett remarked
that her young lady had brought that foreign nurse
home with her two years ago, on her return from a

Continental excursion; that she was treated almost as well as a governess, and had nothing to do but walk out with the baby and chatter French with Master Charles; 'and,' added Mrs Barrett, 'she says there are many Englishwomen in foreign families as well placed as she.'

I stored up this piece of casual information, as careful housewives store seemingly worthless shreds and fragments for which their prescient minds anticipate a possible use some day. Before I left my old friend, she gave me the address of a respectable old-fashioned inn in the city, which, she said, my uncles used to frequent in former days.

In going to London, I ran less risk and evinced less enterprise than the reader may think. In fact, the distance was only fifty miles. My means would suffice both to take me there, to keep me a few days, and also to bring me back if I found no inducement to stay. I regarded it as a brief holiday, permitted for once to work-weary faculties, rather than as an adventure of life and death. There is nothing like taking all you do at a moderate estimate: it keeps mind and body tranquil; whereas grandiloquent notions are apt to hurry both into fever.

Fifty miles were then a day's journey, (for I speak of a time gone by: my hair which till a late period withstood the frosts of time, lies now, at last white, under a white cap, like snow beneath snow.) About nine o'clock of a wet February night I reached London.

My reader, I know, is one who would not thank me for an elaborate reproduction of poetic first impressions; and it is well, inasmuch as I had neither time nor mood to cherish such; arriving as I did late, on a dark, raw, and rainy evening, in a Babylon and a wilderness of which the vastness and the strangeness tried to the utmost any powers of clear thought and steady self-possession with which, in the absence of more brilliant faculties, Nature might have gifted me.

When I left the coach, the strange speech of the cabmen and others waiting round, seemed to me odd as a foreign tongue. I had never before heard the English language chopped up in that way. However, I managed to understand and to be understood, so far as to get myself and trunk safely conveyed to the old inn whereof I had the address. How difficult, how oppressive, how puzzling seemed my flight! In London for the first time; at an inn for the first time; tired with travelling; confused with darkness; palsied with cold; unfurnished with either experience or advice to tell me how to act, and yet – to act obliged.

Into the hands of Common-sense I confided the matter. Common-sense, however, was as chilled and bewildered as all my other faculties, and it was only under the spur of an inexorable necessity that she spasmodically executed her trust. Thus urged, she paid the porter: considering the crisis, I did not blame her too much that she was hugely cheated; she asked the waiter for a room; she timorously called for the chambermaid; what is far more, she bore, without being wholly overcome, a highly supercilious style of demeanour from that young lady, when she appeared.

I recollect this same chambermaid was a pattern of town prettiness and smartness. So trim her waist, her cap, her dress – I wondered how they had all been manufactured. Her speech had an accent which in its mincing glibness seemed to rebuke mine as by authority; her spruce attire flaunted an easy scorn at my plain country garb.

'Well, it can't be helped,' I thought, 'and then the scene is new, and the circumstances; I shall gain good.'

Maintaining a very quiet manner towards this arrogant little maid, and subsequently observing the same towards the parsonic-looking, black-coated, white-neckclothed waiter, I got civility from them ere long. I believe at first they thought I was a servant; but in a little while they changed their minds, and hovered in a doubtful state between patronage and politeness.

I kept up well till I had partaken of some refreshment, warmed myself by a fire, and was fairly shut into my room; but, as I sat down by the bed and rested my head and arms on the pillow, a terrible oppression overcame me. All at once my position rose on me like a ghost. Anomalous; desolate, almost blank of hope, it stood. What was I doing here alone in great London? What should I do on the morrow? What prospects had I in life? What friends had I on earth? Whence did I come? Whither should I go? What should I do?

I wet the pillow, my arms, and my hair, with rushing tears. A dark interval of most bitter thought followed this burst; but I did not regret the step taken, nor wish to retract it. A strong, vague persuasion, that it was better to go forward than backward, and that I *could* go forward – that a way, however narrow and difficult, would in time open, predominated over other feelings: its influence hushed them so far, that at last I became sufficiently tranquil to be able to say my prayers and seek my couch. I had just extinguished my candle and lain down, when a deep, low, mighty tone swung through the night. At first I knew it not; but it was uttered twelve times, and at the twelfth colossal hum and trembling knell, I said: 'I lie in the shadow of St Paul's.'

3

London

THE NEXT DAY was the first of March, and when I awoke, rose, and opened my curtain, I saw the risen sun struggling through fog. Above my head, above the house-tops, co-elevate almost with the clouds, I saw a solemn, orbed mass, dark-blue and dim – THE DOME. While I looked, my inner self moved; my spirit shook its always-fettered wings half loose; I had a sudden feeling as if I, who had never yet truly lived, were at last about to taste life: in that morning my soul grew as fast as Jonah's gourd.

'I did well to come,' I said, proceeding to dress with speed and care. 'I like the spirit of this great London which I feel around me. Who but a coward would pass his whole life in hamlets, and for ever abandon his faculties to the eating rust of obscurity?'

Being dressed, I went down, not travel-worn and

exhausted, but tidy and refreshed. When the waiter came in with my breakfast, I managed to accost him sedately, yet cheerfully; we had ten minutes' discourse, in the course of which we became usefully known to each other.

He was a gray-haired, elderly man; and, it seemed, had lived in his present place twenty years. Having ascertained this, I was sure he must remember my two uncles, Charles and Wilmot, who, fifteen years ago, were frequent visitors here. I mentioned their names; he recalled them perfectly, and with respect. Having intimated my connection, my position in his eyes was henceforth clear, and on a right footing. He said I was like my uncle Charles: I suppose he spoke truth, because Mrs Barrett was accustomed to say the same thing. A ready and obliging courtesy now replaced his former uncomfortably doubtful manner: henceforth I need no longer be at a loss for a civil answer to a sensible question.

The street on which my little sitting-room window looked was narrow, perfectly quiet, and not dirty: the few passengers were just such as one sees in provincial towns: here was nothing formidable; I felt sure I might venture out alone.

Having breakfasted, out I went. Elation and pleasure were in my heart: to walk alone in London seemed of itself an adventure. Presently I found myself in Paternoster-row – classic ground this. I entered a bookseller's shop, kept by one Jones; I bought a little book – a piece of extravagance I could ill afford; but I thought I would one day give or send it to Mrs Barrett. Mr Jones, a dried-in man of business, stood behind his desk; he seemed one of the greatest, and I one of the happiest, of beings.

Prodigious was the amount of life I lived that morning. Finding myself before St Paul's, I went in; I mounted to the dome: I saw thence London, with its river, and its bridges, and its churches; I saw antique Westminster, and the green Temple Gardens, with sun upon them, and a glad, blue sky of early spring above; and, between them and it, not too dense a cloud of haze.

Descending, I went wandering whither chance might lead, in a still ecstacy of freedom and enjoyment; and I got – I know not how – I got into the heart of city life. I saw and felt London at last: I got into the Strand; I went up Cornhill; I mixed with the life passing along; I dared the perils of crossings. To do this, and to do it utterly alone, gave me, perhaps an irrational, but a real pleasure. Since those days, I have seen the West-end, the parks, the fine squares; but I love the city far better. The city seems so much more in earnest: its business, its rush, its roar, are such serious things, sights, and sounds. The city is getting its living – the West-end but enjoying its pleasure. At the West-end you may be amused, but in the city you are deeply excited.

Faint, at last, and hungry (it was years since I had felt such healthy hunger), I returned, about two o'clock, to my dark, old, and quiet inn. I dined on two dishes – a plain joint, and vegetables; both seemed excellent (how much better than the small, dainty messes Miss Marchmont's cook used to send up to my kind, dead mistress and me, and to the discussion of which we could not bring half an appetite between us). Delightfully tired, I lay down on three chairs for an hour (the room did not boast a sofa). I slept, then I woke and thought for two hours.

My state of mind, and all accompanying circumstances, were just now such as most to favour the adoption of a new, resolute, and daring – perhaps desperate – line of action. I had nothing to lose. Unutterable loathing of a desolate existence past forbade return. If I failed in what I now designed to undertake, who, save myself, would suffer? If I died far away from – home, I was going to say, but I had no home – from England, then, who would weep?

I might suffer; I was inured to suffering: death itself had not, I thought, those terrors for me which it has for the softly reared. I had, ere this, looked on the thought of death with a quiet eye. Prepared, then, for any consequences, I formed a project.

That same evening I obtained from my friend, the waiter, information respecting the sailing of vessels for a certain continental port, Boue-Marine. No time, I found, was to be lost: that very night I must take my berth. I might, indeed, have waited till the morning before going on board, but would not run the risk of being too late.

'Better take your berth at once ma'am,' counselled the waiter. I agreed with him, and having discharged my bill, and acknowledged my friend's services at a rate which I now know was princely, and which in his eyes must have seemed absurd – and indeed, while pocketing the cash, he smiled a faint smile which intimated his opinion of the donor's *savoir-faire* – he proceeded to call a coach. To the driver he also recommended me, giving at the same time an injunction about taking me, I think, to the wharf, and not leaving me to the watermen; which that functionary promised to observe, but failed in keeping his promise. On the contrary, he offered me up as oblation, served me as a dripping roast, making me alight in the midst of a throng of watermen.

This was an uncomfortable crisis. It was a dark night. The coachman instantly drove off as soon as he had got his fare; the watermen commenced a struggle for me and my trunk. Their oaths I hear at this moment: they shook my philosophy more than did the night, or the isolation, or the strangeness of the scene. One laid hands on my trunk. I looked on and waited quietly; but when another laid hands on me, I spoke up, shook off his touch, stepped at once into a boat, desired austerely that the trunk should be placed beside me – 'Just there,' – which was instantly done; for the owner of the boat I had chosen became now an ally: I was rowed off.

Black was the river as a torrent of ink: lights glanced on it from the piles of building round, ships rocked on its bosom. They rowed me up to several vessels; I read by lantern-light their names painted in great, white letters on a dark ground. 'The Ocean,' 'The Phoenix,' 'The Consort,' 'The Dolphin,' were passed in turn; but 'The Vivid' was my ship, and it seemed she lay further down.

Down the sable flood we glided; I thought of the Styx, and of Charon rowing some solitary soul to the Land of Shades. Amidst the strange scene, with a chilly wind blowing in my face, and midnight-clouds dropping rain above my head; with two rude rowers for companions, whose insane oaths still tortured my ear, I asked myself if I was wretched or terrified. I was neither. Often in my life have I been far more so under comparatively safe circumstances. 'How is this?' said I. 'Methinks I am animated and alert, instead of being depressed and apprehensive?' I could not tell how it was.

'THE VIVID' started out, white and glaring, from the black night at last. 'Here you are!' said the water-man, and instantly demanded six shillings.

'You ask too much,' I said. He drew off from the vessel and swore he would not embark me till I paid it.

A young man, the steward as I found afterwards, was looking over the ship's side; he grinned a smile in anticipation of the coming contest; to disappoint him, I paid the money. Three times that afternoon I had given crowns where I should have given shillings; but I consoled myself with the reflection, 'It is the price of experience.'

'They've cheated you!' said the steward exultantly when I got on board. I answered phlegmatically that 'I knew it,' and went below.

A stout, handsome, and showy woman was in the ladies' cabin; I asked to be shown my berth; she looked hard at me, muttered something about its being unusual for passengers to come on board at that hour, and seemed disposed to be less than civil. What a face she had – so comely – so insolent and so selfish!

'Now that I am on board, I shall certainly stay here,' was my answer. 'I will trouble you to show me my berth.'

She complied, but sullenly. I took off my bonnet, arranged my things, and lay down. Some difficulties had been passed through; a sort of victory was won: my homeless, anchorless, unsupported mind had again leisure for a brief repose: till the 'Vivid' arrived in harbour, no further action would be required of me, but then . . . Oh! I could not look forward. Harassed, exhausted, I lay in a half-trance.

The stewardess talked all night; not to me, but to

the young steward, her son and her very picture. He passed in and out of the cabin continually: they disputed, they quarrelled, they made it up again twenty times in the course of the night. She professed to be writing a letter home, – she said to her father; she read passages of it aloud, heeding me no more than a stock – perhaps she believed me asleep: several of these passages appeared to comprise family secrets, and bore special reference to one 'Charlotte,' a younger sister who, from the bearing of the epistle, seemed to be on the brink of perpetrating a romantic and imprudent match; loud was the protest of this elder lady against the distasteful union. The dutiful son laughed his mother's correspondence to scorn. She defended it, and raved at him. They were a strange pair. She might be thirty-nine or forty, and was buxom and blooming as a girl of twenty. Hard, loud, vain and vulgar, her mind and body alike seemed brazen and imperishable. I should think, from her childhood, she must have lived in public stations; and in her youth might very likely have been a bar-maid.

Towards morning her discourse ran on a new theme: 'the Watsons,' a certain expected family-party of passengers, known to her, it appeared, and by her much esteemed on account of the handsome profit realized in their fees. She said, 'it was as good as a little fortune to her whenever this family crossed.'

At dawn all were astir, and by sunrise the passengers came on board. Boisterous was the welcome given by the stewardess to the 'Watsons,' and great was the bustle made in their honour. They were four in number, two males and two females. Besides them, there was but one other passenger – a young lady, whom a gentlemanly, though languid-looking man escorted. The two groups offered a marked contrast. The Watsons were doubtless rich people, for they had the confidence of conscious wealth in their bearing; the women – youthful both of them, and one perfectly handsome, as far as physical beauty went – were dressed richly, gaily, and absurdly out of character for the circumstances. Their bonnets with bright flowers, their velvet cloaks and silk dresses seemed better suited for park or promenade than for a damp packet-deck. The men were of low stature, plain, fat, and vulgar; the oldest, plainest, greasiest, broadest, I soon found was the husband – the bridegroom I suppose, for she was very young – of the beautiful girl. Deep was my amazement at this discovery; and deeper still when I perceived that, instead of being desperately wretched in such a union, she was gay even to giddiness. 'Her laughter,' I reflected, 'must be the mere frenzy of despair.' And even while this thought was crossing my mind, as I stood leaning quiet and solitary against the ship's side, she came tripping up to me, an utter stranger, with a camp stool in her hand, and smiling a smile of which the levity puzzled and startled me, though it showed a perfect set of perfect teeth, she offered me the accommodation of this piece of furniture. I declined it, of course with all the courtesy I could put into my manner; she danced off heedless and lightsome. She must have been good-natured; but what had made her marry that individual, who was at least as much like an oil-barrel as a man?

The other lady-passenger, with the gentleman-companion, was quite a girl, pretty and fair; her simple print dress, untrimmed straw-bonnet, and large shawl, gracefully worn, formed a costume plain to quakerism: yet, for her, becoming enough. Before the gentleman quitted her, I observed him throwing a glance of scrutiny over all the passengers, as if to ascertain in what company his charge would be left. With a most dissatisfied air did his eye turn from the ladies with the gay flowers: he looked at me, and then he spoke to his daughter, niece, or whatever she was; she also glanced in my direction, and slightly curled her short, pretty lip. It might be myself, or it might be my homely mourning-habit that elicited this mark of contempt; more likely both. A bell rang; her father (I afterwards knew that it was her father) kissed her and returned to land. The packet sailed.

Foreigners say that it is only English girls who can thus be trusted to travel alone, and deep is their wonder at the daring confidence of English parents and guardians. As for the 'jeunes Miss,' by some their intrepidity is pronounced masculine and 'inconvenant,' others regard them as the passive victims of an educational and theological system which wantonly dispenses with proper 'surveillance.' Whether this particular young lady was of the sort that can the most safely be left unwatched, I do not know: or rather did not *then* know; but it soon appeared that the dignity of solitude was not to her taste. She paced the deck once or twice backwards and forwards; she looked with a little sour air of disdain at the flaunting silks and velvets, and the bears which thereon danced attendance, and eventually she approached me and spoke.

'Are you fond of a sea-voyage?' was her question.

I explained that my *fondness* for a sea-voyage had yet to undergo the test of experience: I had never made one.

'Oh how charming!' cried she. 'I quite envy you the novelty: first impressions, you know, are so pleasant. Now I have made so many, I quite forget the first: I am quite *blasée* about the sea and all that.'

I could not help smiling.

'Why do you laugh at me?' she inquired, with a frank testiness that pleased me better than her other talk.

'Because you are so young to be *blasée* about anything.'

'I am seventeen' (a little piqued).

'You hardly look sixteen. Do you like travelling alone?'

'Bah! I care nothing about it. I have crossed the Channel ten times, alone; but then I take care never to be long alone: I always make friends.'

'You will scarcely make many friends this voyage, I think' (glancing at the Watson-group, who were now laughing and making a great deal of noise on deck).

'Not of those odious men and women,' said she: 'such people should be steerage passengers. Are you going to school?'

'No.'

'Where are you going?'

'I have not the least idea – beyond, at least, the Port of Boue-Marine.'

She stared, then carelessly ran on:

'I am going to school. Oh the number of foreign schools I have been at in my life! And yet I am quite an ignoramus. I know nothing – nothing in the world – I assure you; except that I play and dance beautifully, – and French and German of course I know, to speak; but I can't read or write them very well. Do you know they wanted me to translate a page of an easy German book into English the other day, and I couldn't do it. Papa was so mortified: he says it looks as if M. de Bassompierre – my god-papa, who pays all my school-bills – had thrown away all his money. And then, in matters of information – in history, geography, arithmetic, and so on, I am quite a baby; and I write English so badly – such spelling and grammar, they tell me. Into the bargain I have quite forgotten my religion; they call me a Protestant, you know, but really I am not sure whether I am one or not: I don't well know the difference between Romanism and Protestantism. However, I don't in the least care for that. I was a Lutheran once at Bonn – dear Bonn! – charming Bonn! – where there were so many handsome students. Every nice girl in our school had an admirer; they knew our hours for walking out, and almost always passed us on the promenade: 'Schönes Mädchen,' we used to hear them say. I was excessively happy at Bonn!'

'And where are you now?' I inquired.

'Oh! at – *chose*,' said she.

Now Miss Ginevra Fanshawe (such was this young person's name) only substituted this word '*chose*' in temporary oblivion of the real name. It was a habit she had: '*chose*' came in at every turn in her conversation – the convenient substitute for any missing word in any language she might chance at the time to be speaking. French girls often do the like; from them she had caught the custom. '*Chose*,' however, I found, in this instance, stood for Villette – the great capital of the great kingdom of Labassecour.

'Do you like Villette?' I asked.

'Pretty well. The natives, you know, are intensely stupid and vulgar; but there are some nice English families.'

'Are you in a school?'

'Yes.'

'A good one?'

'Oh no! horrid: but I go out every Sunday, and care nothing about the *maîtresses* or the *professeurs*, or the *élèves*, and send lessons *au diable*; (one daren't say that in English, you know, but it sounds quite right in French,) and thus I get on charmingly . . . You are laughing at me again?'

'No – I am only smiling at my own thoughts.'

'What are they?' (without waiting for an answer) – 'Now *do* tell me where you are going.'

'Where Fate may lead me. My business is to earn a living where I can find it.'

'To earn!' (in consternation) 'are you poor then?'

'As poor as Job.'

(After a pause) 'Bah! how unpleasant! But *I* know what it is to be poor: they are poor enough at home – papa and mama, and all of them. Papa is called Captain Fanshawe; he is an officer on half-pay, but well-descended, and some of our connections are great enough; but my uncle and god-papa de Bassompierre, who lives in France, is the only one that helps us: he educates us girls. I have five sisters and three brothers. By-and-by we are to marry – rather elderly gentlemen, I suppose, with cash: papa and mama manage that. My sister Augusta is married now to a man much older-looking than papa. Augusta is very beautiful – not in my style – but dark; her husband, Mr Davies, had the yellow fever in India, and he is still the colour of a guinea; but then he is rich, and Augusta has her carriage and establishment, and we all think she has done perfectly well. Now this is better than "earning a living," as you say. By the way, are you clever?'

'No – not at all.'

'You can play, sing, speak three or four languages?'

'By no means.'

'Still I think you are clever' (a pause and a yawn). 'Shall you be sea-sick?'

'Shall you?'

'Oh, immensely! as soon as ever we get in sight of the sea: I begin, indeed, to feel it already. I shall go below; and won't I order about that fat, odious stewardess. Heureusement je sais faire aller mon monde.' Down she went.

It was not long before the other passengers followed her: throughout the afternoon I remained on deck alone. When I recall the tranquil, and even happy mood in which I passed those hours, and remember, at the same time, the position in which I was placed: its hazardous – some would have said its hopeless – character; I feel that, as –

> Stone walls do not a prison make,
> Nor iron bars – a cage.

so peril, loneliness, an uncertain future, are not oppressive evils, so long as the frame is healthy and the faculties are employed; so long, especially, as Liberty lends us her wings, and Hope guides us by her star.

4

Declaration

A SPLENDID MIDSUMMER shone over England: skies so pure, suns so radiant as were then seen in long succession, seldom favour, even singly, our wave-girt land. It was as if a band of Italian days had come from the South, like a flock of glorious passenger birds, and lighted to rest them on the cliffs of Albion. The hay was all got in; the fields round Thornfield were green and shorn; the roads white and baked; the trees were in their dark prime: hedge and wood, full-leaved and deeply tinted, contrasted well with the sunny hue of the cleared meadows between.

On Midsummer-eve, Adèle, weary with gathering wild strawberries in Hay-Lane half the day, had gone to bed with the sun. I watched her drop asleep, and when I left her I sought the garden.

It was now the sweetest hour of the twenty-four:–
'Day its fervid fires had wasted,' and dew fell cool on
panting plain and scorched summit. Where the sun
had gone down in simple state – pure of the pomp of
clouds – spread a solemn purple, burning with the
light of red jewel and furnace flame at one point, on
one hill-peak, and extending high and wide, soft and
still softer, over half heaven. The east had its own
charm of fine, deep blue, and its own modest gem, a
rising and solitary star: soon it would boast the moon;
but she was yet beneath the horizon.

I walked a while on the pavement; but a subtle,
well-known scent – that of a cigar – stole from some
window; I saw the library casement open a hand-
breadth; I knew I might be watched thence; so I went
apart into the orchard. No nook in the grounds more
sheltered and more Eden-like; it was full of trees, it
bloomed with flowers: a very high wall shut it out from
the court, on one side; on the other, a beech avenue
screened it from the lawn. At the bottom was a sunk
fence; its sole separation from lonely fields: a winding
walk, bordered with laurels and terminating in a giant
horse-chesnut, circled at the base by a seat, led down
to the fence. Here one could wander unseen. While
such honey-dew fell, such silence reigned, such gloam-
ing gathered, I felt as if I could haunt such shade for
ever: but in threading the flower and fruit-parterres at
the upper part of the enclosure, enticed there by the

light the now-rising moon casts on this more open quarter, my step is stayed – not by sound, not by sight, but once more by a warning fragrance.

Sweet-briar and southernwood, jasmine, pink, and rose have long been yielding their evening sacrifice of incense: this new scent is neither of shrub nor flower; it is – I know it well – it is Mr Rochester's cigar. I look round and I listen. I see trees laden with ripening fruit. I hear a nightingale warbling in a wood half a mile off; no moving form is visible, no coming step audible; but that perfume increases: I must flee. I make for the wicket leading to the shrubbery, and I see Mr Rochester entering. I step aside into the ivy recess; he will not stay long: he will soon return whence he came, and if I sit still he will never see me.

But no – eventide is as pleasant to him as to me, and this antique garden as attractive; and he strolls on, now lifting the gooseberry-tree branches to look at the fruit, large as plums, with which they are laden; now taking a ripe cherry from the wall; now stooping towards a knot of flowers, either to inhale their fragrance or to admire the dew-beads on their petals. A great moth goes humming by me; it alights on a plant at Mr Rochester's foot: he sees it, and bends to examine it.

'Now, he has his back towards me,' thought I, 'and he is occupied too; perhaps, if I walk softly, I can slip away unnoticed.'

I trode on an edging of turf that the crackle of the pebbly gravel might not betray me: he was standing among the beds at a yard or two distant from where I had to pass; the moth apparently engaged him. 'I shall get by very well,' I meditated. As I crossed his shadow, thrown long over the garden by the moon, not yet risen high, he said quietly without turning:–

'Jane, come and look at this fellow.'

I had made no noise: he had not eyes behind – could his shadow feel? I started at first, and then I approached him.

'Look at his wings,' said he, 'he reminds me rather of a West Indian insect; one does not often see so large and gay a night-rover in England: there! he is flown.'

The moth roamed away. I was sheepishly retreating also: but Mr Rochester followed me, and when we reached the wicket, he said:–

'Turn back: on so lovely a night it is a shame to sit in the house; and surely no one can wish to go to bed while sunset is thus at meeting with moonrise.'

It is one of my faults, that though my tongue is sometimes prompt enough at an answer, there are times when it sadly fails me in framing an excuse; and always the lapse occurs at some crisis, when a facile word or plausible pretext is specially wanted to get me out of painful embarrassment. I did not like to walk at this hour alone with Mr Rochester in the shadowy orchard; but I could not find a reason to allege for leaving him. I followed with lagging step, and thoughts busily bent on discovering a means of extrication; but he himself looked so composed and so grave also, I became ashamed of feeling any confusion: the evil – if evil existent or prospective there was – seemed to lie with me only; his mind was unconscious and quiet.

'Jane,' he recommenced, as we entered the laurel-walk, and slowly strayed down in the direction of the sunk fence and the horse-chesnut, 'Thornfield is a pleasant place in summer, is it not?'

'Yes, sir.'

'You must have become in some degree attached to the house, – you, who have an eye for natural beauties, and a good deal of the organ of Adhesiveness?'

'I am attached to it, indeed.'

'And, though I don't comprehend how it is, I perceive you have acquired a degree of regard for that foolish little child Adèle, too; and even for simple dame Fairfax?'

'Yes, sir; in different ways, I have an affection for both.'

'And would be sorry to part with them?'

'Yes.'

'Pity!' he said, and sighed and paused. 'It is always the way of events in this life,' he continued presently: 'no sooner have you got settled in a pleasant resting-place, than a voice calls out to you to rise and move on, for the hour of repose is expired.'

'Must I move on, sir?' I asked. 'Must I leave Thornfield?'

'I believe you must, Jane. I am sorry, Janet, but I believe indeed you must.'

This was a blow: but I did not let it prostrate me.

'Well, sir, I shall be ready when the order to march comes.'

'It is come now – I must give it tonight.'

'Then you are going to be married, sir?'

'Ex-act-ly – pre-cise-ly: with your usual acuteness, you have hit the nail straight on the head.'

'Soon, sir?'

'Very soon, my – that is, Miss Eyre: and you'll remember, Jane, the first time I, or Rumour, plainly intimated to you that it was my intention to put my old bachelor's neck into the sacred noose, to enter into the holy estate of matrimony – to take Miss Ingram to my bosom, in short (she's an extensive armful: but that's not to the point – one can't have too much of such a very excellent thing as my beautiful Blanche): well, as I was saying – listen to me, Jane! You're not turning your head to look after more moths, are you? That was only a ladyclock, child, 'flying away home.' I wish to remind you that it was you who first said to me, with that discretion I respect in you – with that foresight, prudence, and humility which befit your responsible and dependent position – that in case I married Miss Ingram – both you and little Adèle had better trot forthwith. I pass over the sort of slur conveyed in this suggestion on the character of my beloved; indeed, when you are far away, Janet, I'll try to forget it: I shall notice only its wisdom; which is such that I have made it my law of action. Adèle must go to school; and you, Miss Eyre, must get a new situation.'

'Yes, sir, I will advertise immediately: and meantime, I suppose—' I was going to say, 'I suppose I may stay here, till I find another shelter to betake myself to:' but I stopped, feeling it would not do to risk a long sentence, for my voice was not quite under command.

'In about a month I hope to be a bridegroom,' continued Mr Rochester; 'and in the interim I shall myself look out for employment and an asylum for you.'

'Thank you, sir; I am sorry to give—'

'Oh, no need to apologize! I consider that when a dependant does her duty as well as you have done yours, she has a sort of claim upon her employer for any little assistance he can conveniently render her; indeed I have already, through my future mother-in-law, heard of a place that I think will suit: it is to undertake the education of the five daughters of Mrs Dionysius O'Gall of Bitternutt Lodge, Connaught, Ireland. You'll like Ireland, I think: they're such warm-hearted people there, they say.'

'It is a long way off, sir.'

'No matter – a girl of your sense will not object to the voyage or the distance.'

'Not the voyage, but the distance: and then the sea is a barrier—'

'From what, Jane?'

'From England and from Thornfield: and—'

'Well?'

'From *you*, sir.'

I said this almost involuntarily; and, with as little sanction of free will, my tears gushed out. I did not cry so as to be heard, however; I avoided sobbing. The thought of Mrs O'Gall and Bitternutt Lodge struck cold to my heart; and colder the thought of all the brine and foam, destined, as it seemed, to rush between me and the master at whose side I now walked; and coldest the remembrance of the wider ocean – wealth, caste, custom intervened between me and what I naturally and inevitably loved.

'It is a long way,' I again said.

'It is to be sure; and when you get to Bitternutt Lodge, Connaught, Ireland, I shall never see you again, Jane: that's morally certain. I never go over to Ireland, not having myself much of a fancy for the country. We have been good friends, Jane; have we not?'

'Yes, sir.'

'And when friends are on the eve of separation, they like to spend the little time that remains to them close to each other. Come – we'll talk over the voyage and the parting quietly, half an hour or so, while the stars enter into their shining life up in heaven yonder: here is the chestnut-tree; here is the bench at its old roots. Come, we will sit there in peace tonight, though we should never more be destined to sit there together.' He seated me and himself.

'It is a long way to Ireland, Janet, and I am sorry to send my little friend on such weary travels: but if I can't do better, how is it to be helped? Are you anything akin to me, do you think, Jane?'

I could risk no sort of answer by this time: my heart was full.

'Because,' he said, 'I sometimes have a queer feeling with regard to you – especially when you are near me, as now: it is as if I had a string somewhere under my left ribs, tightly and inextricably knotted to a similar string situated in the corresponding quarter of your little frame. And if that boisterous channel, and two hundred miles or so of land come broad between us, I am afraid that cord of communion will be snapt; and then I've a nervous notion I should take to bleeding inwardly. As for you, – you'd forget me.'

'That I *never* should, sir: you know—' impossible to proceed.

'Jane, do you hear that nightingale singing in the wood? Listen!'

In listening, I sobbed convulsively; for I could

repress what I endured no longer; I was obliged to yield, and I was shaken from head to foot with acute distress. When I did speak, it was only to express an impetuous wish that I had never been born, or never come to Thornfield.

'Because you are sorry to leave it?'

The vehemence of emotion, stirred by grief and love within me, was claiming mastery, and struggling for full sway; and asserting a right to predominate: to overcome, to live, rise, and reign at last; yes, – and to speak.

'I grieve to leave Thornfield: I love Thornfield:– I love it, because I have lived in it a full and delightful life, – momentarily at least. I have not been trampled on. I have not been petrified. I have not been buried with inferior minds, and excluded from every glimpse of communion with what is bright and energetic, and high. I have talked, face to face, with what I reverence; with what I delight in, – with an original, a vigorous, an expanded mind. I have known you, Mr Rochester; and it strikes me with terror and anguish to feel I absolutely must be torn from you for ever. I see the necessity of departure; and it is like looking on the necessity of death.'

'Where do you see the necessity?' he asked, suddenly.

'Where? You, sir, have placed it before me.'

'In what shape?'

'In the shape of Miss Ingram; a noble and beautiful woman, – your bride.'

'My bride! What bride? I have no bride!'

'But you will have.'

'Yes; – I will! – I will!' He set his teeth.

'Then I must go:– you have said it yourself.'

'No: you must stay! I swear it – and the oath shall be kept.'

'I tell you I must go!' I retorted, roused to something like passion. 'Do you think I can stay to become nothing to you? Do you think I am an automaton? – a machine without feelings? and can bear to have my morsel of bread snatched from my lips, and my drop of living water dashed from my cup? Do you think, because I am poor, obscure, plain, and little, I am soulless and heartless? – You think wrong! – I have as much soul as you, – and full as much heart! And if God had gifted me with some beauty, and much wealth, I should have made it as hard for you to leave me, as it is now for me to leave you. I am not talking to you now through the medium of custom, conventionalities, nor even of mortal flesh:– it is my spirit that addresses your spirit; just as if both had passed through the grave, and we stood at God's feet, equal, – as we are!'

'As we are!' repeated Mr Rochester – 'so,' he added, enclosing me in his arms, gathering me to his breast, pressing his lips on my lips: 'so, Jane!'

'Yes, so, sir,' I rejoined: 'and yet not so; for you are

a married man – or as good as a married man, and wed to one inferior to you – to one with whom you have no sympathy – whom I do not believe you truly love; for I have seen and heard you sneer at her. I would scorn such a union: therefore I am better than you – let me go!'

'Where, Jane? To Ireland?'

'Yes – to Ireland. I have spoken my mind, and can go anywhere now.'

'Jane, be still; don't struggle so, like a wild, frantic bird that is rending its own plumage in its desperation.'

'I am no bird; and no net ensnares me: I am a free human being with an independent will; which I now exert to leave you.'

Another effort set me at liberty, and I stood erect before him.

'And your will shall decide your destiny,' he said: 'I offer you my hand, my heart, and a share of all my possessions.'

'You play a farce, which I merely laugh at.'

'I ask you to pass through life at my side – to be my second self, and best earthly companion.'

'For that fate you have already made your choice, and must abide by it.'

'Jane, be still a few moments; you are over-excited: I will be still too.'

A waft of wind came sweeping down the

laurel-walk, and trembled through the boughs of the chestnut: it wandered away – away – to an indefinite distance – it died. The nightingale's song was then the only voice of the hour: in listening to it, I again wept. Mr Rochester sat quiet, looking at me gently and seriously. Some time passed before he spoke; he at last said:–

'Come to my side, Jane, and let us explain and understand one another.'

'I will never again come to your side: I am torn away now, and cannot return.'

'But, Jane, I summon you as my wife: it is you only I intend to marry.'

I was silent: I thought he mocked me.

'Come, Jane – come hither.'

'Your bride stands between us.'

He rose, and with a stride reached me.

'My bride is here,' he said, again drawing me to him, 'because my equal is here, and my likeness. Jane, will you marry me?'

Still I did not answer, and still I writhed myself from his grasp: for I was still incredulous.

'Do you doubt me, Jane?'

'Entirely.'

'You have no faith in me?'

'Not a whit.'

'Am I a liar in your eyes?' he asked passionately. 'Little sceptic, you *shall* be convinced. What love have

I for Miss Ingram? None: and that you know. What love has she for me? None: as I have taken pains to prove: I caused a rumour to reach her that my fortune was not a third of what was supposed, and after that I presented myself to see the result; it was coldness both from her and her mother. I would not – I could not – marry Miss Ingram. You – you strange – you almost unearthly thing! – I love as my own flesh. You – poor and obscure, and small and plain as you are – I entreat to accept me as a husband.'

'What, me!' I ejaculated: beginning in his earnestness – and especially in his incivility – to credit his sincerity: 'me who have not a friend in the world but you – if you are my friend: not a shilling but what you have given me?'

'You, Jane. I must have you for my own – entirely my own. Will you be mine? Say yes, quickly.'

'Mr Rochester, let me look at your face: turn to the moonlight.'

'Why?'

'Because I want to read your countenance; turn!'

'There: you will find it scarcely more legible than a crumpled, scratched page. Read on: only make haste, for I suffer.'

His face was very much agitated and very much flushed, and there were strong workings in the features, and strange gleams in the eyes.

'Oh, Jane, you torture me!' he exclaimed. 'With

that searching and yet faithful and generous look, you torture me!'

'How can I do that? If you are true, and your offer real, my only feelings to you must be gratitude and devotion – they cannot torture.'

'Gratitude!' he ejaculated; and added wildly – 'Jane, accept me quickly. Say, Edward – give me my name – Edward – I will marry you.'

'Are you in earnest? – Do you truly love me? – Do you sincerely wish me to be your wife?'

'I do; and if an oath is necessary to satisfy you, I swear it.'

'Then, sir, I will marry you.'

'Edward – my little wife!'

'Dear Edward!'

'Come to me – come to me entirely now,' said he: and added, in his deepest tone, speaking in my ear as his cheek was laid on mine, 'Make my happiness – I will make yours.'

'God pardon me!' he subjoined ere long; 'and man meddle not with me: I have her, and will hold her.'

'There is no one to meddle, sir. I have no kindred to interfere.'

'No – that is the best of it,' he said. And if I had loved him less I should have thought his accent and look of exultation savage: but, sitting by him, roused from the nightmare of parting – called to the paradise of union – I thought only of the bliss given me to drink in so abundant a flow. Again and again he said, 'Are you happy, Jane?' And again and again I answered, 'Yes.' After which he murmured, 'It will atone – it will atone. Have I not found her friendless, and cold, and comfortless? Will I not guard, and cherish, and solace her? Is there not love in my heart, and constancy in my resolves? It will expiate at God's tribunal. I know my Maker sanctions what I do. For the world's judgment – I wash my hands thereof. For man's opinion – I defy it.'

But what had befallen the night? The moon was not yet set, and we were all in shadow: I could scarcely see my master's face, near as I was. And what ailed the chestnut-tree? it writhed and groaned; while wind roared in the laurel-walk, and came sweeping over us.

'We must go in,' said Mr Rochester: 'the weather changes. I could have sat with thee till morning, Jane.'

'And so,' thought I, 'could I with you.' I should have said so, perhaps, but a livid, vivid spark leapt out of a cloud at which I was looking, and there was a crack, a crash, and a close rattling peal; and I thought only of hiding my dazzled eyes against Mr Rochester's shoulder.

The rain rushed down. He hurried me up the walk, through the grounds, and into the house; but we were quite wet before we could pass the threshold.

He was taking off my shawl in the hall, and shaking the water out of my loosened hair, when Mrs Fairfax emerged from her room. I did not observe her at first, nor did Mr Rochester. The lamp was lit. The clock was on the stroke of twelve.

'Hasten to take off your wet things,' said he; 'and before you go, good-night – good-night, my darling!'

He kissed me repeatedly. When I looked up, on leaving his arms, there stood the widow, pale, grave, and amazed. I only smiled at her, and ran up stairs. 'Explanation will do for another time,' thought I. Still, when I reached my chamber, I felt a pang at the idea she should even temporarily misconstrue what she had seen. But joy soon effaced every other feeling; and loud as the wind blew, near and deep as the thunder crashed, fierce and frequent as the lightning gleamed, cataract-like as the rain fell during a storm of two hours' duration, I experienced no fear, and little awe. Mr Rochester came thrice to my door in the course of it, to ask if I was safe and tranquil: and that was comfort, that was strength for anything.

Before I left my bed in the morning, little Adèle came running in to tell me that the great horse-chestnut at the bottom of the orchard had been struck by lightning in the night, and half of it split away.

5

Flight

SOME TIME IN the afternoon I raised my head, and looking round and seeing the western sun gilding the sign of its decline on the wall, I asked, 'What am I to do?'

But the answer my mind gave – 'Leave Thornfield at once' – was so prompt, so dread, that I stopped my ears: I said, I could not bear such words now. 'That I am not Edward Rochester's bride is the least part of my woe,' I alleged: 'that I have wakened out of most glorious dreams, and found them all void and vain, is a horror I could bear and master; but that I must leave him decidedly, instantly, entirely, is intolerable. I cannot do it.'

But, then, a voice within me averred that I could do it; and foretold that I should do it. I wrestled with my own resolution: I wanted to be weak that I might avoid the awful passage of further suffering I saw laid out for me; and conscience, turned tyrant, held passion by the throat, told her tauntingly, she had yet but dipped her dainty foot in the slough, and swore that with that arm of iron, he would thrust her down to unsounded depths of agony.

'Let me be torn away, then!' I cried. 'Let another help me!'

'No; you shall tear yourself away, none shall help you: you shall, yourself, pluck out your right eye: yourself cut off your right hand: your heart shall be the victim; and you, the priest, to transfix it.'

I rose up suddenly, terror-struck at the solitude which so ruthless a judge haunted, – at the silence which so awful a voice filled. My head swam as I stood erect: I perceived that I was sickening from excitement and inanition: neither meat nor drink had passed my lips that day, for I had taken no breakfast. And, with a strange pang, I now reflected that, long as I had been shut up here, no message had been sent to ask how I was, or to invite me to come down: not even little Adèle had tapped at the door; not even Mrs Fairfax had sought me. 'Friends always forget those whom fortune forsakes,' I murmured, as I undrew the bolt and passed out. I stumbled over an obstacle: my head was still dizzy, my sight was dim, and my limbs were feeble. I could not soon recover myself. I fell, but not on to the ground: an out-stretched arm caught me; I looked up – I was supported by Mr Rochester, who sat in a chair across my chamber threshold.

'You come out at last,' he said. 'Well, I have been waiting for you long, and listening: yet not one movement have I heard, nor one sob: five minutes more of that death-like hush, and I should have forced the lock like a burglar. So, you shun me? – you shut yourself up and grieve alone! I would rather you had come and upbraided me with vehemence. You are passionate: I expected a scene of some kind. I was prepared for the hot rain of tears; only I wanted them to be shed on my breast: now a senseless floor has received them, or your drenched handkerchief. But I err: you have not wept at all! I see a white cheek and a faded eye, but no trace of tears. I suppose, then, your heart has been weeping blood?

'Well, Jane; not a word of reproach? Nothing bitter – nothing poignant? Nothing to cut a feeling or sting a passion? You sit quietly where I have placed you, and regard me with a weary, passive look.

'Jane, I never meant to wound you thus. If the man who had but one little ewe lamb that was dear to him as a daughter, that ate of his bread and drank of his cup, and lay in his bosom, had by some mistake slaughtered it at the shambles, he would not have rued his bloody blunder more than I now rue mine. Will you ever forgive me?'

Reader! – I forgave him at the moment, and on

the spot. There was such deep remorse in his eye, such true pity in his tone, such manly energy in his manner; and, besides, there was such unchanged love in his whole look and mien – I forgave him all: yet not in words, not outwardly; only at my heart's core.

'You know I am a scoundrel, Jane?' ere long he inquired wistfully – wondering, I suppose, at my continued silence and tameness: the result rather of weakness than of will.

'Yes, sir.'

'Then tell me so roundly and sharply – don't spare me.'

'I cannot: I am tired and sick. I want some water.' He heaved a sort of shuddering sigh, and taking me in his arms, carried me down stairs. At first I did not know to what room he had borne me; all was cloudy to my glazed sight: presently I felt the reviving warmth of a fire; for, summer as it was, I had become icy cold in my chamber. He put wine to my lips; I tasted it and revived; then I ate something he offered me, and was soon myself. I was in the library – sitting in his chair – he was quite near. 'If I could go out of life now, without too sharp a pang, it would be well for me,' I thought; 'then I should not have to make the effort of cracking my heart-strings in rending them from among Mr Rochester's. I must leave him, it appears. I do not want to leave him – I cannot leave him.'

'How are you now, Jane?'

'Much better, sir: I shall be well soon.'

'Taste the wine again, Jane.'

I obeyed him; then he put the glass on the table, stood before me, and looked at me attentively. Suddenly he turned away, with an inarticulate exclamation, full of passionate emotion of some kind; he walked fast through the room and came back: he stooped towards me as if to kiss me; but I remembered caresses were now forbidden. I turned my face away, and put his aside.

'What! – How is this?' he exclaimed hastily. 'Oh, I know! you won't kiss the husband of Bertha Mason? You consider my arms filled, and my embraces appropriated?'

'At any rate, there is neither room nor claim for me, sir.'

'Why, Jane? I will spare you the trouble of much talking: I will answer for you – because I have a wife already, you would reply. – I guess rightly?'

'Yes.'

'If you think so, you must have a strange opinion of me: you must regard me as a plotting profligate – a base and low rake who has been simulating disinterested love in order to draw you into a snare deliberately laid, and strip you of honour, and rob you of self-respect. What do you say to that? I see you can say nothing: in the first place, you are faint, still, and have enough to do to draw your breath; in the second place, you cannot yet accustom yourself to accuse and revile me; and, besides, the flood-gates of tears are opened, and they would rush out if you spoke much; and you have no desire to expostulate, to upbraid, to make a scene: you are thinking how *to act – talking*, you consider, is of no use. I know you – I am on my guard.'

'Sir, I do not wish to act against you,' I said; and my unsteady voice warned me to curtail my sentence.

'Not in *your* sense of the word but in *mine*, you are scheming to destroy me. You have as good as said that I am a married man – as a married man you will shun me, keep out of my way: just now you have refused to kiss me. You intend to make yourself a complete stranger to me; to live under this roof only as Adèle's governess: if ever I say a friendly word to you; if ever a friendly feeling inclines you again to me, you will say, – 'That man had nearly made me his mistress: I must be ice and rock to him;' and ice and rock you will accordingly become.'

I cleared and steadied my voice to reply: 'All is changed about me, sir; I must change too – there is no doubt of that: and to avoid fluctuations of feeling, and continual combats with recollections and associations, there is only one way – Adèle must have a new governess, sir.'

'Oh, Adèle will go to school – I have settled that already, nor do I mean to torment you with the hideous associations and recollections of Thornfield

Hall – this accursed place – this tent of Achan – this insolent vault, offering the ghastliness of living death to the light of the open sky – this narrow stone hell, with its one real fiend, worse than a legion of such as we imagine. – Jane, you shall not stay here, nor will I. I was wrong ever to bring you to Thornfield Hall, knowing as I did how it was haunted. I charged them to conceal from you, before I ever saw you, all knowledge of the curse of the place; merely because I feared Adèle never would have a governess to stay if she knew with what inmate she was housed, and my plans would not permit me to remove the maniac elsewhere – though I possess an old house, Ferndean Manor, even more retired and hidden than this, where I could have lodged her safely enough, had not a scruple about the unhealthiness of the situation, in the heart of a wood, made my conscience recoil from the arrangement. Probably those damp walls would soon have eased me of her charge: but to each villain his own vice; and mine is not a tendency to indirect assassination, even of what I most hate.

'Concealing the mad-woman's neighbourhood, from you, however, was something like covering a child with a cloak, and laying it down near a upas-tree: that demon's vicinage is poisoned, and always was. But I'll shut up Thornfield Hall: I'll nail up the front door, and board the lower windows; I'll give Mrs Poole two hundred a year to live here with *my wife*, as you term that fearful hag: Grace will do much for money, and she shall have her son, the keeper at Grimsby Retreat, to bear her company and be at hand to give her aid, in the paroxysms, when *my wife* is prompted by her familiar to burn people in their beds at night, to stab them, to bite their flesh from their bones, and so on' –

'Sir,' I interrupted him, 'you are inexorable for that unfortunate lady: you speak of her with hate – with vindictive antipathy. It is cruel – she cannot help being mad.'

'Jane, my little darling (so I will call you, for so you are), you don't know what you are talking about; you misjudge me again: it is not because she is mad I hate her. If you were mad, do you think I should hate you?'

'I do indeed, sir.'

'Then you are mistaken, and you know nothing about me, and nothing about the sort of love of which I am capable. Every atom of your flesh is as dear to me as my own: in pain and sickness it would still be dear. Your mind is my treasure, and if it were broken, it would be my treasure still: if you raved, my arms should confine you, and not a strait waistcoat – your grasp, even in fury, would have a charm for me: if you flew at me as wildly as that woman did this morning, I should receive you in an embrace, at least as fond as it would be restrictive. I should not shrink from you with disgust as I did from her: in your quiet moments you should have no watcher and no nurse but me; and I could hang over you with untiring tenderness, though you gave me no smile in return; and never weary of gazing into your eyes, though they had no longer a ray of recognition for me. – But why do I follow that train of ideas? I was talking of removing you from Thornfield. All, you know, is prepared for prompt departure: tomorrow you shall go. I only ask you to endure one more night under this roof, Jane; and then, farewell to its miseries and terrors for ever! I have a place to repair to, which will be a secure sanctuary from hateful reminiscences, from unwelcome intrusion – even from falsehood and slander.'

'And take Adèle with you, sir,' I interrupted; 'she will be a companion for you.'

'What do you mean, Jane? I told you I would send Adèle to school: and what do I want with a child for a companion? and not my own child, – a French dancer's bastard. Why do you importune me about her? I say, why do you assign Adèle to me for a companion?'

'You spoke of a retirement, sir; and retirement and solitude are dull: too dull for you.'

'Solitude! solitude!' he reiterated, with irritation. 'I see I must come to an explanation. I don't know what sphynx-like expression is forming in your countenance. *You* are to share my solitude. Do you understand?'

I shook my head: it required a degree of courage, excited as he was becoming, even to risk that mute sign of dissent. He had been walking fast about the room, and he stopped, as if suddenly rooted to one spot. He looked at me long and hard: I turned my eyes from him, fixed them on the fire, and tried to assume and maintain a quiet, collected aspect.

'Now for the hitch in Jane's character,' he said at last, speaking more calmly than from his look I had expected him to speak. 'The reel of silk has run smoothly enough so far; but I always knew there would come a knot and a puzzle: here it is. Now for vexation, and exasperation, and endless trouble! By God! I long to exert a fraction of Samson's strength, and break the entanglement like tow!'

He recommenced his walk: but soon again stopped, and this time just before me.

'Jane! will you hear reason?' (he stooped and approached his lips to my ear) 'because, if you won't, I'll try violence.' His voice was hoarse; his look that of a man who is just about to burst an insufferable bond and plunge headlong into wild licence. I saw that in another moment, and with one impetus of frenzy more, I should be able to do nothing with him. The present – the passing second of time – was all I had in which to control and restrain him: a movement of repulsion, flight, fear, would have sealed my doom, – and his. But I was not afraid: not in the least. I felt an inward power; a sense of influence, which supported me. The crisis was perilous; but not without its charm: such as the Indian, perhaps, feels when he slips over the rapid in his canoe. I took hold of his clenched hand; loosened the contorted fingers; and said to him, soothingly, –

'Sit down; I'll talk to you as long as you like, and hear all you have to say, whether reasonable or unreasonable.'

He sat down: but he did not get leave to speak directly. I had been struggling with tears for some time: I had taken great pains to repress them, because I knew he would not like to see me weep. Now, however, I considered it well to let them flow as freely and as long as they liked. If the flood annoyed him, so much the better. So I gave way and cried heartily.

Soon I heard him earnestly entreating me to be composed. I said I could not while he was in such a passion.

'But I am not angry, Jane: I only love you too well; and you had steeled your little pale face with such a resolute, frozen look, I could not endure it. Hush, now, and wipe your eyes.'

His softened voice announced that he was subdued; so I, in my turn, became calm. Now he made an effort to rest his head on my shoulder: but I would not permit it. Then he would draw me to him: no.

'Jane! Jane!' he said – in such an accent of bitter

sadness, it thrilled along every nerve I had; 'you don't love me, then? It was only my station, and the rank of my wife, that you valued? Now that you think me disqualified to become your husband, you recoil from my touch as if I were some toad or ape.'

These words cut me: yet what could I do or say? I ought probably to have done or said nothing: but I was so tortured by a sense of remorse at thus hurting his feelings, I could not control the wish to drop balm where I had wounded.

'I *do* love you,' I said, 'more than ever: but I must not show or indulge the feeling: and this is the last time I must express it.'

'The last time, Jane! What! do you think you can live with me, and see me daily, and yet, if you still love me, be always cold and distant?'

'No, sir; that I am certain I could not; and therefore I see there is but one way: but you will be furious if I mention it.'

'Oh, mention it! If I storm, you have the art of weeping.'

'Mr Rochester, I must leave you.'

'For how long, Jane? For a few minutes, while you smooth your hair – which is somewhat dishevelled; and bathe your face – which looks feverish?'

'I must leave Adèle and Thornfield. I must part with you for my whole life: I must begin a new exist-ence amongst strange faces and strange scenes.'

'Of course: I told you you should. I pass over the madness about parting from me. You mean you must become a part of me. As to the new existence, it is all right: you shall yet be my wife: I am not married. You shall be Mrs Rochester – both virtually and nom- inally. I shall keep only to you so long as you and I live. You shall go to a place I have in the south of France: a white-washed villa on the shores of the Mediterra- nean. There you shall live a happy, and guarded, and most innocent life. Never fear that I wish to lure you into error – to make you my mistress. Why do you shake your head? Jane, you must be reasonable; or in truth I shall again become frantic.'

His voice and hand quivered: his large nostrils dilated; his eye blazed: still I dared to speak:–

'Sir, your wife is living: that is a fact acknowledged this morning by yourself. If I lived with you as you desire, I should then be your mistress: to say other- wise is sophistical – is false.'

'Jane, I am not a gentle-tempered man – you forget that: I am not long-enduring; I am not cool and dis- passionate. Out of pity to me and yourself, put your finger on my pulse, feel how it throbs, and – beware!'

He bared his wrist, and offered it to me: the blood was forsaking his cheek and lips, they were growing livid; I was distressed on all hands. To agitate him thus deeply, by a resistance he so abhorred, was cruel: to yield was out of the question. I did what human beings do instinctively when they are driven to utter extremity – looked for aid to one higher than man: the words 'God help me!' burst involuntarily from my lips.

'I am a fool!' cried Mr Rochester, suddenly. 'I keep telling her I am not married, and do not explain to her why. I forget she knows nothing of the character of that woman, or of the circumstances attending my infernal union with her. Oh, I am certain Jane will agree with me in opinion, when she knows all that I know! Just put your hand in mine, Janet – that I may have the evidence of touch as well as sight, to prove you are near me – and I will in a few words show you the real state of the case. Can you listen to me?'

. . .

'YOU SEE NOW how the case stands – do you not?' he continued. 'After a youth and manhood passed half in unutterable misery and half in dreary solitude, I have for the first time found what I can truly love – I have found *you*. You are my sympathy – my better self – my good angel – I am bound to you with a strong attachment. I think you good, gifted, lovely: a fervent, a solemn passion is conceived in my heart; it leans to you, draws you to my centre and spring of life, wraps my existence about you – and, kindling in pure, powerful flame, fuses you and me in one.

'It was because I felt and knew this, that I resolved to marry you. To tell me that I had already a wife is empty mockery: you know now that I had but a hideous demon. I was wrong to attempt to deceive you; but I feared a stubbornness that exists in your character. I feared early instilled prejudice: I wanted to have you safe before hazarding confidences. This was cowardly: I should have appealed to your noble-ness and magnanimity at first, as I do now – opened to you plainly my life of agony – described to you my hunger and thirst after a higher and worthier existence – shown to you, not my *resolution* (that word is weak) but my resistless *bent* to love faithfully and well, where I am faithfully and well loved in return. Then I should have asked you to accept my pledge of fidelity, and to give me yours: Jane – give it me now.'

A pause.

'Why are you silent, Jane?'

I was experiencing an ordeal: a hand of fiery iron grasped my vitals. Terrible moment: full of struggle, blackness, burning! Not a human being that ever lived could wish to be loved better than I was loved; and him who thus loved me I absolutely worshipped: and I must renounce love and idol. One drear word comprised my intolerable duty – 'Depart!'

'Jane, you understand what I want of you? Just this promise – "I will be yours, Mr Rochester."'

'Mr Rochester, I will *not* be yours.'

Another long silence.

'Jane!' recommenced he, with a gentleness that

broke me down with grief, and turned me stone-cold with ominous terror – for this still voice was the pant of a lion rising – 'Jane, do you mean to go one way in the world, and to let me go another?'

'I do.'

'Jane' (bending towards and embracing me), 'do you mean it now?'

'I do.'

'And now?' softly kissing my forehead and cheek.

'I do—' extricating myself from restraint rapidly and completely.

'Oh, Jane, this is bitter! This – this is wicked. It would not be wicked to love me.'

'It would to obey you.'

A wild look raised his brows – crossed his features: he rose; but he forbore yet. I laid my hand on the back of a chair for support: I shook, I feared – but I resolved.

'One instant, Jane. Give one glance to my horrible life when you are gone. All happiness will be torn away with you. What then is left? For a wife I have but the maniac up stairs: as well might you refer me to some corpse in yonder churchyard. What shall I do, Jane? Where turn for a companion, and for some hope?'

'Do as I do: trust in God and yourself. Believe in heaven. Hope to meet again there.'

'Then you will not yield?'

'No.'

'Then you condemn me to live wretched, and to die accursed?' His voice rose.

'I advise you to live sinless; and I wish you to die tranquil.'

'Then you snatch love and innocence from me? You fling me back on lust for a passion – vice for an occupation?'

'Mr Rochester, I no more assign this fate to you than I grasp at it for myself. We were born to strive and endure – you as well as I: do so. You will forget me before I forget you.'

'You make me a liar by such language: you sully my honour. I declared I could not change: you tell me to my face I shall change soon. And what a distortion in your judgment, what a perversity in your ideas, is proved by your conduct! Is it better to drive a fellow-creature to despair than to transgress a mere human law – no man being injured by the breach? for you have neither relatives nor acquaintances whom you need fear to offend by living with me.'

This was true: and while he spoke my very Conscience and Reason turned traitors against me, and charged me with crime in resisting him. They spoke almost as loud as Feeling: and that clamoured wildly. 'Oh, comply!' it said. 'Think of his misery; think of his danger – look at his state when left alone; remember his headlong nature; consider the recklessness following on despair – soothe him; save him; love him; tell him you love him and will be his. Who in the world cares for *you*? or who will be injured by what you do?'

Still indomitable was the reply – 'I care for myself. The more solitary, the more friendless, the more unsustained I am, the more I will respect myself. I will keep the law given by God; sanctioned by man. I will hold to the principles received by me when I was sane, and not mad – as I am now. Laws and principles are not for the times when there is no temptation: they are for such moments as this, when body and soul rise in mutiny against their rigour; stringent are they; inviolate they shall be. If at my individual convenience I might break them, what would be their worth? They have a worth – so I have always believed; and if I cannot believe it now, it is because I am insane – quite insane: with my veins running fire, and my heart beating faster than I can count its throbs. Preconceived opinions, foregone determinations, are all I have at this hour to stand by: there I plant my foot.'

I did. Mr Rochester, reading my countenance, saw I had done so. His fury was wrought to the highest: he must yield to it for a moment, whatever followed; he crossed the floor and seized my arm, and grasped my waist. He seemed to devour me with his flaming glance: physically, I felt, at the moment, powerless as stubble exposed to the draught and glow of a furnace – mentally, I still possessed my soul, and with it the certainty of ultimate safety. The soul, fortunately, has an interpreter – often an unconscious, but still a truthful interpreter – in the eye. My eye rose to his; and while I looked in his fierce face, I gave an involuntary sigh: his gripe was painful, and my over-tasked strength almost exhausted.

'Never,' said he, as he ground his teeth, 'never was anything at once so frail and so indomitable. A mere reed she feels in my hand!' (And he shook me with the force of his hold.) 'I could bend her with my finger and thumb: and what good would it do if I bent, if I uptore, if I crushed her? Consider that eye: consider the resolute, wild, free thing looking out of it, defying me, with more than courage – with a stern triumph. Whatever I do with its cage, I cannot get at it – the savage, beautiful creature! If I tear, if I rend the slight prison, my outrage will only let the captive loose. Conqueror I might be of the house; but the inmate would escape to heaven before I could call myself possessor of its clay dwelling-place. And it is you, spirit – with will and energy, and virtue and purity – that I want: not alone your brittle frame. Of yourself, you could come with soft flight and nestle against my heart, if you would: seized against your will you will elude the grasp like an essence – you will vanish ere I inhale your fragrance. Oh! come, Jane, come!'

As he said this, he released me from his clutch, and only looked at me. The look was far worse to resist than the frantic strain: only an idiot, however, would have succumbed now. I had dared and baffled his fury; I must elude his sorrow: I retired to the door.

'You are going, Jane?'

'I am going, sir.'

'You are leaving me?'

'Yes.'

'You will not come? – You will not be my comforter, my rescuer? – My deep love, my wild woe, my frantic prayer, are all nothing to you?'

What unutterable pathos was in his voice! How hard it was to reiterate firmly, 'I am going.'

'Jane!'

'Mr Rochester!'

'Withdraw, then – I consent – but remember, you leave me here in anguish. Go up to your own room; think over all I have said, and, Jane, cast a glance on my sufferings – think of me.'

He turned away; he threw himself on his face on the sofa. 'Oh, Jane! my hope – my love – my life!' broke in anguish from his lips. Then came a deep, strong sob.

I had already gained the door: but, reader, I walked back – walked back as determinedly as I had retreated. I knelt down by him; I turned his face from the cushion to me; I kissed his cheek; I smoothed his hair with my hand.

'God bless you, my dear master!' I said. 'God keep you from harm and wrong – direct you, solace you – reward you well for your past kindness to me.'

'Little Jane's love would have been my best reward,' he answered: 'without it, my heart is broken. But Jane will give me her love: yes – nobly, generously.'

Up the blood rushed to his face; forth flashed the fire from his eyes; erect he sprang; he held his arms out; but I evaded the embrace, and at once quitted the room.

'Farewell!' was the cry of my heart, as I left him. Despair added, 'Farewell, for ever!'

THAT NIGHT I never thought to sleep; but a slumber fell on me as soon as I lay down in bed. I was transported in thought to the scenes of childhood: I dreamt I lay in the red-room at Gateshead; that the night was dark, and my mind impressed with strange fears. The light that long ago had struck me into syncope, recalled in this vision, seemed glidingly to mount the wall, and tremblingly to pause in the centre of the obscured ceiling. I lifted up my head to look: the roof resolved to clouds, high and dim; the gleam was such as the moon imparts to vapours, she is about to sever. I watched her come – watched with the strangest anticipation; as though some word of doom were to be written on her disk. She broke forth as never moon yet burst from cloud: a hand first penetrated the sable folds and waved them away; then, not a moon, but a white human form shone in the azure, inclining a glorious brow earthward. It gazed and gazed on me. It spoke to my spirit: immeasurably distant was the tone, yet so near, it whispered in my heart –

'My daughter, flee temptation!'

'Mother, I will.'

So I answered after I had waked from the trance-like dream. It was yet night, but July nights are short: soon after midnight, dawn comes. 'It cannot be too early to commence the task I have to fulfil,' thought I. I rose: I was dressed; for I had taken off nothing but my shoes. I knew where to find in my drawers some linen, a locket, a ring. In seeking these articles, I encountered the beads of a pearl necklace Mr Rochester had forced me to accept a few days ago. I left that; it was not mine: it was the visionary bride's, who had melted in air. The other articles I made up in a parcel; my purse, containing twenty shillings (it was all I had), I put in my pocket: I tied on my straw bonnet, pinned my shawl, took the parcel and my slippers, which I would not put on yet, and stole from my room.

'Farewell, kind Mrs Fairfax!' I whispered, as I glided past her door. 'Farewell, my darling Adèle!' I said, as I glanced towards the nursery. No thought could be admitted of entering to embrace her. I had to deceive a fine ear: for aught I knew, it might now be listening.

I would have got past Mr Rochester's chamber without a pause; but my heart momentarily stopping its beat at that threshold, my foot was forced to stop also. No sleep was there: the inmate was walking restlessly from wall to wall; and again and again he sighed while I listened. There was a heaven – a temporary heaven – in this room for me, if I chose: I had but to go in and to say –

'Mr Rochester, I will love you and live with you through life till death,' and a fount of rapture would spring to my lips. I thought of this.

That kind master, who could not sleep now, was waiting with impatience for day. He would send for me in the morning; I should be gone. He would have me sought for: vainly. He would feel himself forsaken; his love rejected: he would suffer; perhaps grow desperate. I thought of this too. My hand moved towards the lock: I caught it back, and glided on.

Drearily I wound my way down stairs: I knew what I had to do, and I did it mechanically. I sought the key of the side-door in the kitchen; I sought, too, a phial of oil and a feather; I oiled the key and the lock. I got some water, I got some bread: for perhaps I should have to walk far; and my strength, sorely shaken of late, must not break down. All this I did without one sound. I opened the door, passed out, shut it softly. Dim dawn glimmered in the yard. The great gates were closed and locked; but a wicket in one of them was only latched. Through that I departed: it, too, I shut; and now I was out of Thornfield.

6

Refusal

PERHAPS YOU THINK I had forgotten Mr Rochester, reader, amidst these changes of place and fortune. Not for a moment. His idea was still with me; because it was not a vapour sunshine could disperse; nor a sand-traced effigy storms could wash away: it was a name graven on a tablet, fated to last as long as the marble it inscribed. The craving to know what had become of him followed me everywhere; when I was at Morton, I re-entered my cottage every evening to think of that; and now at Moor-House, I sought my bed-room each night to brood over it.

In the course of my necessary correspondence with Mr Briggs about the will, I had inquired if he knew anything of Mr Rochester's present residence and state of health; but, as St John had conjectured, he was quite ignorant of all concerning him. I then wrote to Mrs Fairfax, entreating information on the subject. I had calculated with certainty on this step answering my end: I felt sure it would elicit an early answer. I was astonished when a fortnight passed without reply; but when two months wore away, and day after day the post arrived and brought nothing for me, I fell a prey to the keenest anxiety.

I wrote again: there was a chance of my first letter having missed. Renewed hope followed renewed effort: it shone like the former for some weeks, then, like it, it faded, flickered: not a line, not a word reached me. When half a year wasted in vain expectancy, my hope died out: and then I felt dark indeed.

A fine spring shone round me, which I could not enjoy. Summer approached; Diana tried to cheer me: she said I looked ill, and wished to accompany me to the sea-side. This St John opposed; he said I did not want dissipation, I wanted employment; my present life was too purposeless, I required an aim; and, I suppose, by way of supplying deficiencies, he prolonged still further my lessons in Hindostanee, and grew more urgent in requiring their accomplishment: and I, like a fool, never thought of resisting him – I could not resist him.

One day I had come to my studies in lower spirits than usual; the ebb was occasioned by a poignantly felt disappointment: Hannah had told me in the morning there was a letter for me, and when I went down to take it, almost certain that the long looked-for tidings were vouchsafed me at last, I found only an unimportant note from Mr Briggs on business. The bitter check had wrung from me some tears; and now as I sat poring over the crabbed characters and flourishing tropes of an Indian scribe, my eyes filled again.

St John called me to his side to read; in attempting to do this my voice failed me: words were lost in sobs. He and I were the only occupants of the parlour: Diana was practising her music in the drawing-room, Mary was gardening – it was a very fine May-day, clear, sunny, and breezy. My companion expressed no surprise at this emotion, nor did he question me as to its cause; he only said:–

'We will wait a few minutes, Jane, till you are more composed.' And while I smothered the paroxysm with all haste, he sat calm and patient, leaning on his desk and looking like a physician watching with the eye of science an expected and fully-understood crisis in a patient's malady. Having stifled my sobs, wiped my eyes, and muttered something about not being very well that morning, I resumed my task, and succeeded in completing it. St John put away my books and his, locked his desk, and said:–

'Now, Jane, you shall take a walk; and with me.'

'I will call Diana and Mary.'

'No. I want only one companion this morning, and that must be you: put on your things; go out by the kitchen door; take the road towards the head of Marsh-Glen: I will join you in a moment.'

I know no medium: I never in my life have known any medium in my dealings with positive, hard characters, antagonistic to my own, between absolute submission and determined revolt. I have always faithfully observed the one, up to the very moment of bursting, sometimes with volcanic vehemence, into the other; and as neither present circumstances warranted, nor my present mood inclined me to mutiny, I observed careful obedience to St John's directions; and in ten minutes I was treading the wild track of the glen, side by side with him.

The breeze was from the west: it came over the hills, sweet with scents of heath and rush; the sky was of stainless blue; the stream descending the ravine, swelled with past spring rains, poured along plentiful and clear, catching golden gleams from the sun, and sapphire tints from the firmament. As we advanced and left the track, we trod a soft turf, mossy fine and emerald green, minutely enamelled with a tiny white flower, and spangled with a star-like yellow blossom: the hills, meantime, shut us quite in; for the glen, towards its head, wound to their very core.

'Let us rest here,' said St John, as we reached the first stragglers of a battalion of rocks, guarding a sort of pass, beyond which the beck rushed down a waterfall; and where, still a little further, the mountain shook off turf and flower, had only heath for raiment, and crag for gem – where it exaggerated the wild to the savage, and exchanged the fresh for the frowning – where it guarded the forlorn hope of solitude, and a last refuge for silence.

I took a seat: St John stood near me. He looked up the pass and down the hollow; his glance wandered away with the stream, and returned to traverse the unclouded heaven which coloured it: he removed his hat, let the breeze stir his hair and kiss his brow. He seemed in communion with the genius of the haunt: with his eye he bade farewell to something.

'And I shall see it again,' he said aloud, 'in dreams, when I sleep by the Ganges: and again, in a more remote hour – when another slumber overcomes me – on the shore of a darker stream.'

Strange words of a strange love! An austere patriot's passion for his fatherland! He sat down; for half an hour we never spoke; neither he to me nor I to him: that interval past, he recommenced:–

'Jane, I go in six weeks: I have taken my berth in an East Indiaman which sails on the twentieth of June.'

'God will protect you; for you have undertaken His work,' I answered.

'Yes,' said he, 'there is my glory and joy. I am the servant of an infallible master. I am not going out under human guidance, subject to the defective laws and erring control of my feeble fellow-worms: my king, my lawgiver, my captain, is the All-perfect. It seems strange to me that all round me do not burn to enlist under the same banner, – to join in the same enterprise.'

'All have not your powers; and it would be folly for the feeble to wish to march with the strong.'

'I do not speak to the feeble, or think of them: I address only such as are worthy of the work, and competent to accomplish it.'

'Those are few in number, and difficult to discover.'

'You say truly: but when found, it is right to stir them up – to urge and exhort them to the effort – to show them, what their gifts are, and why they were given – to speak Heaven's message in their ear, – to offer them, direct from God, a place in the ranks of his chosen.'

'If they are really qualified for the task, will not their own hearts be the first to inform them of it?'

I felt as if an awful charm was framing round and gathering over me: I trembled to hear some fatal word spoken which would at once declare and rivet the spell.

'And what does *your* heart say?' demanded St John.

'My heart is mute, – my heart is mute,' I answered, struck and thrilled.

'Then I must speak for it,' continued the deep, relentless voice. 'Jane, come with me to India: come as my helpmeet and fellow-labourer.'

The glen and sky spun round: the hills heaved! It was as if I had heard a summons from Heaven – as if a visionary messenger, like him of Macedonia, had enounced, 'Come over and help us!' But I was no apostle, could not behold the herald, – I could not receive his call.

'Oh, St John!' I cried, 'have some mercy!'

I appealed to one who, in the discharge of what he believed his duty, knew neither mercy nor remorse. He continued:–

'God and nature intended you for a missionary's wife. It is not personal, but mental endowments they have given you: you are formed for labour, not for love. A missionary's wife you must – shall be. You shall be mine: I claim you – not for my pleasure, but for my Sovereign's service.'

'I am not fit for it: I have no vocation,' I said.

He had calculated on these first objections: he was not irritated by them. Indeed, as he leaned back against the crag behind him, folded his arms on his chest, and fixed his countenance, I saw he was prepared for a long and trying opposition, and had taken in a stock of patience to last him to its close – resolved, however, that that close should be conquest for him.

'Humility, Jane,' said he, 'is the groundwork of Christian virtues: you say right that you are not fit for the work. Who is fit for it? Or who, that ever was truly called, believed himself worthy of the summons? I, for instance, am but dust and ashes. With St Paul, I acknowledge myself the chiefest of sinners: but I do not suffer this sense of my personal vileness to daunt me. I know my Leader: that He is just as well as mighty; and while He has chosen a feeble instrument to perform a great task, He will, from the boundless stores of His providence, supply the inadequacy of the means to the end. Think like me, Jane – trust like me. It is the Rock of Ages I ask you to lean on: do not doubt but it will bear the weight of your human weakness.'

'I do not understand a missionary life: I have never studied missionary labours.'

'There, I, humble as I am, can give you the aid you want: I can set your task from hour to hour; stand by you always; help you from moment to moment. This I could do in the beginning: soon (for I know your powers) you would be as strong and apt as myself, and would not require my help.'

'But my powers – where are they for this undertaking? I do not feel them. Nothing speaks or stirs in me while you talk. I am sensible of no light kindling – no life quickening – no voice counselling or cheering. Oh, I wish I could make you see how much my mind is at this moment like a rayless dungeon, with one shrinking fear fettered in its depths – the fear of being persuaded by you to attempt what I cannot accomplish!'

'I have an answer for you – hear it. I have watched

you ever since we first met: I have made you my study for ten months. I have proved you in that time by sundry tests: and what have I seen and elicited? In the village school I found you could perform well, punctually, uprightly, labour uncongenial to your habits and inclinations; I saw you could perform it with capacity and tact: you could win while you controlled. In the calm with which you learnt you had become suddenly rich, I read a mind clear of the vice of Demas:– lucre had no undue power over you. In the resolute readiness with which you cut your wealth into four shares, keeping but one to yourself, and relinquishing the three others to the claim of abstract justice, I recognised a soul that revelled in the flame and excitement of sacrifice. In the tractability with which, at my wish, you forsook a study in which you were interested, and adopted another because it interested me; in the untiring assiduity with which you have since persevered in it – in the unflagging energy and unshaken temper with which you have met its difficulties – I acknowledge the complement of the qualities I seek. Jane, you are docile, diligent, disinterested, faithful, constant, and courageous; very gentle, and very heroic: cease to mistrust yourself – I can trust you unreservedly. As a conductress of Indian schools, and a helper amongst Indian women, your assistance will be to me invaluable.'

My iron shroud contracted round me; persuasion

advanced with slow sure step. Shut my eyes as I would, these last words of his succeeded in making the way, which had seemed blocked up, comparatively clear. My work, which had appeared so vague, so hopelessly diffuse, condensed itself as he proceeded, and assumed a definite form under his shaping hand. He waited for an answer. I demanded a quarter of an hour to think, before I again hazarded a reply.

'Very willingly,' he rejoined: and rising, he strode a little distance up the pass, threw himself down on a swell of heath, and there lay still.

'I *can* do what he wants me to do: I am forced to see and acknowledge that,' I meditated – 'That is, if life be spared me. But I feel mine is not the existence to be long protracted under an Indian sun. – What then? He does not care for that: when my time came to die he would resign me, in all serenity and sanctity, to the God who gave me. The case is very plain before me. In leaving England, I should leave a loved but empty land – Mr Rochester is not there: and if he were, what is, what can that ever be to me? My business is to live without him now: nothing so absurd, so weak as to drag on from day to day, as if I were waiting some impossible change in circumstances, which might reunite me to him. Of course (as St John once said) I must seek another interest in life to replace the one lost: is not the occupation he now offers me truly the most glorious man can adopt or God assign?

Is it not, by its noble cares and sublime results, the one best calculated to fill the void left by uptorn affections and demolished hopes? I believe I must say, Yes – and yet I shudder. Alas! If I join St John, I abandon half myself: if I go to India, I go to premature death. And how will the interval between leaving England for India, and India for the grave, be filled? Oh, I know well! That, too, is very clear to my vision. By straining to satisfy St John till my sinews ache, I *shall* satisfy him – to the finest central point and farthest outward circle of his expectations. If I *do* go with him – if I *do* make the sacrifice he urges, I will make it absolutely: I will throw all on the altar – heart, vitals, the entire victim. He will never love me; but he shall approve me: I will show him energies he has not yet seen, resources he has never suspected. Yes: I can work as hard as he can; and with as little grudging.

'Consent, then, to his demand is possible: but for one item – one dreadful item. It is – that he asks me to be his wife, and has no more of a husband's heart for me than that frowning giant of a rock, down which the stream is foaming in yonder gorge. He prizes me as a soldier would a good weapon; and that is all. Unmarried to him, this would never grieve me; but can I let him complete his calculations – coolly put into practice his plans – go through the wedding ceremony? Can I receive from him the bridal ring, endure all the forms of love (which I doubt not he would scrupulously observe) and know that the spirit was quite absent? Can I bear the consciousness that every endearment he bestows is a sacrifice made on principle? No: such a martyrdom would be monstrous. I will never undergo it. As his sister, I might accompany him – not as his wife: I will tell him so.'

I looked towards the knoll: there he lay, still as a prostrate column; his face turned to me: his eye beaming watchful, and keen. He started to his feet, and approached me.

'I am ready to go to India, if I may go free.'

'Your answer requires a commentary,' he said; 'it is not clear.'

'You have hitherto been my adopted brother: I, your adopted sister; let us continue as such: you and I had better not marry.'

He shook his head. 'Adopted fraternity will not do in this case. If you were my real sister it would be different: I should take you, and seek no wife. But as it is, either our union must be consecrated and sealed by marriage, or it cannot exist: practical obstacles oppose themselves to any other plan. Do you not see it, Jane? Consider a moment – your strong sense will guide you.'

I did consider: and still my sense, such as it was, directed me only to the fact that we did not love each other as man and wife should; and therefore it inferred we ought not to marry. I said so. 'St John,' I returned, 'I regard you as a brother – you, me as a sister: so let us continue.'

'We cannot – we cannot,' he answered, with short, sharp determination: 'it would not do. You have said you will go with me to India: remember – you have said that.'

'Conditionally.'

'Well – well. To the main point – the departure with me from England, the co-operation with me in my future labours – you do not object. You have already as good as put your hand to the plough: you are too consistent to withdraw it. You have but one end to keep in view – how the work you have undertaken can best be done. Simplify your complicated interests, feelings, thoughts, wishes, aims; merge all considerations in one purpose: that of fulfilling with effect – with power – the mission of your great Master. To do so, you must have a coadjutor – not a brother; that is a loose tie: but a husband. I, too, do not want a sister: a sister might any day be taken from me. I want a wife: the sole helpmeet I can influence efficiently in life, and retain absolutely till death.'

I shuddered as he spoke: I felt his influence in my marrow – his hold on my limbs.

'Seek one elsewhere than in me, St John: seek one fitted to you.'

'One fitted to my purpose, you mean – fitted to my vocation. Again I tell you it is not the insignificant private individual – the mere man, with the man's selfish senses – I wish to mate: it is the missionary.'

'And I will give the missionary my energies – it is all he wants – but not myself: that would be only adding the husk and shell to the kernel. For them he has no use: I retain them.'

'You cannot – you ought not. Do you think God will be satisfied with half an oblation? Will He accept a mutilated sacrifice? It is the cause of God I advocate: it is under His standard I enlist you. I cannot accept on His behalf a divided allegiance: it must be entire.'

'Oh! I will give my heart to God,' I said, '*You* do not want it.'

I will not swear, reader, that there was not something of repressed sarcasm both in the tone in which I uttered this sentence, and in the feeling that accompanied it. I had silently feared St John till now, because I had not understood him. He had held me in awe, because he had held me in doubt. How much of him was saint, how much mortal, I could not heretofore tell; but revelations were being made in this conference: the analysis of his nature was proceeding before my eyes. I saw his fallibilities: I comprehended them. I understood that, sitting there where I did, on the bank of heath, and with that handsome form before me I sat at the feet of a man, erring as I. The veil fell from his hardness and despotism. Having felt in him the presence of these qualities, I felt his imperfection, and took courage. I was with an equal – one with whom I might argue – one whom, if I saw good, I might resist.

He was silent after I had uttered the last sentence, and I presently risked an upward glance at his countenance. His eye, bent on me, expressed at once stern surprise and keen inquiry. 'Is she sarcastic, and sarcastic to *me*!' it seemed to say. 'What does this signify?'

'Do not let us forget that this is a solemn matter,' he said ere long; 'one of which we may neither think nor talk lightly without sin. I trust, Jane, you are in earnest when you say you will give your heart to God: it is all I want. Once wrench your heart from man, and fix it on your Maker, the advancement of that Maker's spiritual kingdom on earth will be your chief delight and endeavour: you will be ready to do at once whatever furthers that end. You will see what impetus would be given to your efforts and mine by our physical and mental union in marriage: the only union that gives a character of permanent conformity to the destinies and designs of human beings: and, passing over all minor caprices – all trivial difficulties and delicacies of feeling – all scruple about the degree, kind, strength, or tenderness of mere personal inclination – you will hasten to enter into that union at once.'

'Shall I?' I said, briefly; and I looked at his features, beautiful in their harmony, but strangely formidable in their still severity; at his brow, commanding but not open; at his eyes, bright and deep, and searching, but never soft; at his tall, imposing figure; and fancied myself in idea *his wife*. Oh! it would never do! As his curate, his comrade, all would be right: I would cross oceans with him in that capacity; toil under eastern suns, in Asian deserts with him in that office; admire and emulate his courage, and devotion, and vigour; accommodate quietly to his masterhood; smile undisturbed at his ineradicable ambition; discriminate the Christian from the man: profoundly esteem the one, and freely forgive the other. I should suffer often, no doubt, attached to him only in this capacity: my body would be under rather a stringent yoke, but my heart and mind would be free. I should still have my unblighted self to turn to: my natural unenslaved feelings with which to communicate in moments of loneliness. There would be recesses in my mind which would be only mine, to which he never came; and sentiments growing there fresh and sheltered, which his austerity could never blight, nor his measured warrior-march trample down: but as his wife – at his side always, and always restrained, and always checked – forced to keep the fire of my nature continually low, to compel it to burn inwardly and never utter a cry, though the imprisoned flame consumed vital after vital – *this* would be unendurable.

'St John!' I exclaimed, when I had got so far in my meditation.

'Well?' he answered, icily.

'I repeat: I freely consent to go with you as your fellow-missionary; but not as your wife; I cannot marry you and become part of you.'

'A part of me you must become,' he answered steadily; 'otherwise the whole bargain is void. How can I, a man not yet thirty, take out with me to India a girl of nineteen, unless she be married to me? How can we be for ever together – sometimes in solitudes, sometimes amidst savage tribes – and unwed?'

'Very well,' I said shortly; 'under the circumstances, quite as well as if I were either your real sister; or a man and a clergyman like yourself.'

'It is known that you are not my sister; I cannot introduce you as such: to attempt it would be to fasten injurious suspicions on us both. And for the rest, though you have a man's vigorous brain, you have a woman's heart, and – it would not do.'

'It would do,' I affirmed with some disdain, 'perfectly well. I have a woman's heart; but not where you are concerned; for you I have only a comrade's constancy; a fellow-soldier's frankness, fidelity, fraternity, if you like; a neophyte's respect and submission to his hierophant: nothing more – don't fear.'

'It is what I want,' he said, speaking to himself; 'it is just what I want. And there are obstacles in the way: they must be hewn down. Jane you would not repent marrying me; be certain of that; we *must* be married. I repeat it: there is no other way; and undoubtedly enough of love would follow upon marriage to render the union right even in your eyes.'

'I scorn your idea of love,' I could not help saying; as I rose up and stood before him, leaning my back against the rock. 'I scorn the counterfeit sentiment you offer: yes, St John, and I scorn you when you offer it.'

He looked at me fixedly: compressing his well-cut lips while he did so. Whether he was incensed or surprised, or what, it was not easy to tell: he could command his countenance thoroughly.

'I scarcely expected to hear that expression from you,' he said: 'I think I have done and uttered nothing to deserve scorn.'

I was touched by his gentle tone, and overawed by his high, calm mien.

'Forgive me the words, St John: but it is your own fault that I have been roused to speak so unguardedly. You have introduced a topic on which our natures are at variance – a topic we should never discuss: the very name of love is an apple of discord between us – if the reality were required what should we do? How should we feel? My dear cousin, abandon your scheme of marriage – forget it.'

'No,' said he; 'it is a long-cherished scheme, and the only one which can secure my great end: but I shall urge you no further at present. Tomorrow, I leave home for Cambridge: I have many friends there to whom I should wish to say farewell. I shall be absent a fortnight – take that space of time to consider my offer: and do not forget that if you reject it, it is not me you deny, but God. Through my means, He opens to you a noble career; as my wife only can you enter upon it. Refuse to be my wife, and you limit yourself for ever to a track of selfish ease and barren obscurity. Tremble lest in that case you should be numbered with those who have denied the faith and are worse than infidels!'

He had done. Turning from me, he once more –

'Looked to river, looked to hill:'

But this time his feelings were all pent in his heart: I was not worthy to hear them uttered. As I walked by his side homeward, I read well in his iron silence all he felt towards me: the disappointment of an austere and despotic nature, which has met resistance where it expected submission – the disapprobation of a cool, inflexible judgment, which has detected in another feelings and views in which it has no power to sympathize: in short, as a man, he would have wished to coerce me into obedience: it was only as a sincere Christian he bore so patiently with my perversity, and allowed so long a space for reflection and repentance.

That night, after he had kissed his sisters, he thought proper to forget even to shake hands with me; but left the room in silence. I – who, though I had no love, had much friendship for him – was hurt by the marked omission: so much hurt that tears started to my eyes.

'I see you and St John have been quarrelling, Jane,' said Diana, 'during your walk on the moor. But go after him; he is now lingering in the passage, expecting you – he will make it up.'

I have not much pride under such circumstances: I would always rather be happy than dignified; and I ran after him – he stood at the foot of the stairs.

'Good-night, St John,' said I.

'Good-night, Jane,' he replied, calmly.

'Then shake hands,' I added.

What a cold, loose touch he impressed on my fingers! He was deeply displeased by what had occurred that day: cordiality would not warm, nor tears move him. No happy reconciliation was to be had with him – no cheering smile or generous word: but still the Christian was patient and placid; and when I asked him if he forgave me, he answered that he was not in the habit of cherishing the remembrance of vexation; that he had nothing to forgive; not having been offended.

And with that answer, he left me. I would much rather he had knocked me down.

7

Vocation

I CAME AT last to an old and worn flight, and, taking it for granted that this must be the one indicated, I descended them. The street into which they led was indeed narrow, but it contained no inn. On I wandered. In a very quiet and comparatively clean and well-paved street, I saw a light burning over the door of a rather large house, loftier by a storey than those round it. *This* might be the inn at last. I hastened on: my knees now trembled under me: I was getting quite exhausted.

No inn was this. A brass-plate embellished the great Porte-cochère: 'Pensionnat de Demoiselles' was the inscription; and beneath, a name, 'Madame Beck.'

I started. About a hundred thoughts volleyed through my mind in a moment. Yet I planned nothing, and considered nothing: I had not time. Providence said, 'Stop here; this is *your* inn.' Fate took me in her strong hand; mastered my will; directed my actions: I rung the door-bell.

While I waited, I would not reflect. I fixedly looked at the street-stones, where the door-lamp shone, and counted them, and noted their shapes, and the glitter of wet on their angles. I rang again. They opened at last. A bonne in a smart cap stood before me.

'May I see Madame Beck?' I inquired.

I believe if I had spoken French she would not have admitted me; but, as I spoke English, she concluded I was a foreign teacher come on business connected with the Pensionnat, and, even at that late hour, she let me in, without a word of reluctance or a moment of hesitation.

The next moment I sat in a cold, glittering salon, with porcelain stove unlit, and gilded ornaments, and polished floor. A pendule on the mantel-piece struck nine o'clock.

A quarter of an hour passed. How fast beat every pulse in my frame! How I turned cold and hot by turns! I sat with my eyes fixed on the door – a great white folding-door, with gilt mouldings: I watched to see a leaf move and open. All had been quiet: not a mouse had stirred; the white doors were closed and motionless.

'You ayre Engliss?' said a voice at my elbow. I

almost bounded, so unexpected was the sound; so certain had I been of solitude.

No ghost stood beside me, nor anything of spectral aspect; merely a motherly, dumpy little woman, in a large shawl, a wrapping-gown, and a clean, trim night-cap.

I said I was English, and immediately, without further prelude, we fell to a most remarkable conversation. Madame Beck (for Madame Beck it was – she had entered by a little door behind me, and, being shod with the shoes of silence, I had heard neither her entrance nor approach) – Madame Beck had exhausted her command of insular speech when she said, 'You ayre Engliss,' and she now proceeded to work away volubly in her own tongue. I answered in mine. She partly understood me, but as I did not at all understand her – though we made together an awful clamour (anything like madame's gift of utterance I had not hitherto heard or imagined) – we achieved little progress. She rang, ere long, for aid; which arrived in the shape of a 'maîtresse,' who had been partly educated in an Irish convent, and was esteemed a perfect adept in the English language. A bluff little personage this maîtresse was – Labassecourienne from top to toe: and how she did slaughter the speech of Albion! However, I told her a plain tale, which she translated. I told her how I had left my own country, intent on extending my knowledge, and gaining my bread; how I was ready to turn my hand to any useful thing, provided it was not wrong or degrading: how I would be a child's-nurse or a lady's-maid, and would not refuse even housework adapted to my strength. Madame heard this; and, questioning her countenance, I almost thought the tale won her ear:

'Il n'y a que les Anglaises pour ces sortes d'entreprises,' said she: 'sont-elles donc intrépides ces femmes là!'

She asked my name, my age; she sat and looked at me – not pityingly, not with interest: never a gleam of sympathy, or a shade of compassion, crossed her countenance during the interview. I felt she was not one to be led an inch by her feelings: grave and con-siderate, she gazed, consulting her judgment and studying my narrative. A bell rang.

'Voilà pour la prière du soir!' said she, and rose. Through her interpreter, she desired me to depart now, and come back on the morrow; but this did not suit me: I could not bear to return to the perils of darkness and the street. With energy, yet with a col-lected and controlled manner, I said, addressing herself personally, and not the maîtresse:

'Be assured, madame, that by instantly securing my services, your interests will be served and not injured: you will find me one who will wish to give, in her labour, a full equivalent for her wages; and if you hire me, it will be better that I should stay here this night: having no acquaintance in Villette, and not possessing the language of the country, how can I secure a lodging?'

'It is true;' said she, 'but at least you can give me a reference?'

'None.'

She inquired after my luggage: I told her when it would arrive. She mused. At that moment a man's step was heard in the vestibule, hastily proceeding to the outer door. (I shall go on with this part of my tale as if I had understood all that passed; for though it was then scarce intelligible to me, I heard it translated afterwards).

'Who goes out now?' demanded Madame Beck, listening to the tread.

'M. Paul,' replied the teacher. 'He came this evening to give a reading to the first class.'

'The very man I should at this moment most wish to see. Call him.'

The teacher ran to the salon door. M. Paul was summoned. He entered: a small, dark and spare man, in spectacles.

'Mon cousin,' began madame, 'I want your opinion. We know your skill in physiognomy; use it now. Read that countenance.'

The little man fixed on me his spectacles. A resolute compression of the lips, and gathering of the brow, seemed to say that he meant to see through me, and that a veil would be no veil for him.

'I read it,' he pronounced.

'Et qu'en dites vous?'

'Mais – bien des choses,' was the oracular answer.

'Bad or good?'

'Of each kind, without doubt,' pursued the diviner.

'May one trust her word?'

'Are you negotiating a matter of importance?'

'She wishes me to engage her as bonne or gouvernante; tells a tale full of integrity, but gives no reference.'

'She is a stranger?'

'An Englishwoman, as one may see.'

'She speaks French?'

'Not a word.'

'She understands it?'

'No.'

'One may then speak plainly in her presence?'

'Doubtless.'

He gazed steadily. 'Do you need her services?'

'I could do with them. You know I am disgusted with Madame Svini.'

Still he scrutinized. The judgment, when it at last came, was as indefinite as what had gone before it.

'Engage her. If good predominates in that nature, the action will bring its own reward; if evil – eh bien!

ma cousine, ce sera toujours une bonne œuvre.' And with a bow and a 'bon soir,' this vague arbiter of my destiny vanished. And madame did engage me that very night – by God's blessing I was spared the necessity of passing forth again into the lonesome, dreary, hostile street.

8

Madame Beck

BEING DELIVERED INTO the charge of the maîtresse,
I was led through a long, narrow passage into a foreign kitchen, very clean but very strange. It seemed
to contain no means of cooking – neither fireplace
nor oven; I did not understand that the great black
furnace which filled one corner, was an efficient
substitute for these. Surely pride was not already
beginning its whispers in my heart; yet I felt a sense
of relief when, instead of being left in the kitchen, as
I half-anticipated, I was led forward to a small inner
room termed a 'cabinet.' A cook in a jacket, a short
petticoat and sabots, brought my supper: to wit, –
some meat, nature unknown, served in an odd and
acid, but pleasant sauce; some chopped potatoes,
made savoury with, I know not what: vinegar and
sugar, I think; a tartine, or slice of bread and

butter, and a baked pear. Being hungry, I ate and was grateful.

After the 'Prière du Soir,' madame herself came to have another look at me. She desired me to follow her upstairs. Through a series of the queerest little dormitories – which, I heard afterwards, had once been nuns' cells: for the premises were in a part of ancient date – and through the oratory – a long, low, gloomy room, where a crucifix hung, pale, against the wall, and two tapers kept dim vigils – she conducted me to an apartment where three children were asleep in three tiny beds. A heated stove made the air of this room oppressive; and, to mend matters, it was scented with an odour rather strong than delicate: a perfume, indeed, altogether surprising and unexpected under the circumstances, being like the combination of smoke with some spirituous essence – a smell, in short, of whiskey.

Beside a table, on which flared the remnant of a candle guttering to waste in the socket, a coarse woman, heterogeneously clad in a broad-striped showy silk dress and a stuff apron, sat in a chair fast asleep. To complete the picture, and leave no doubt as to the state of matters, a bottle and an empty glass stood at the sleeping beauty's elbow.

Madame contemplated this remarkable tableau with great calm; she neither smiled nor scowled: no impress of anger, disgust, or surprise, ruffled the equality of her grave aspect; she did not even wake the woman. Serenely pointing to a fourth bed, she intimated that it was to be mine, then, having extinguished the candle and substituted for it a night-lamp, she glided through an inner door, which she left ajar: the entrance to her own chamber, a large, well-furnished apartment; as was discernible through the aperture.

My devotions that night were all thanksgiving: strangely had I been led since morning – unexpectedly had I been provided for. Scarcely could I believe that not forty-eight hours had elapsed since I left London, under no other guardianship than that which protects the passenger-bird – with no prospect but the dubious cloud-tracery of hope.

I was a light sleeper; in the dead of night I suddenly awoke. All was hushed, but a white figure stood in the room – Madame in her nightdress. Moving without perceptible sound, she visited the three children in the three beds; she approached me: I feigned sleep, and she studied me long. A small pantomime ensued, curious enough. I dare say she sat a quarter of an hour on the edge of my bed, gazing at my face. She then drew nearer, bent close over me; slightly raised my cap, and turned back the border so as to expose my hair; she looked at my hand lying on the bed-clothes. This done, she turned to the chair where my clothes lay: it was at the foot of the bed. Hearing her touch and lift them, I opened my eyes with precaution, for I own I felt curious to see how far her taste for research would lead her. It led her a good way: every article did she inspect. I divined her motive for this proceeding, viz., the wish to form from the garments a judgment respecting the wearer, her station, means, neatness, &c. The end was not bad, but the means were hardly fair or justifiable. In my dress was a pocket; she fairly turned it inside out: she counted the money in my purse; she opened a little memorandum-book, coolly perused its contents, and took from between the leaves a small plaited lock of Miss Marchmont's grey hair. To a bunch of three keys, being those of my trunk, desk, and work-box, she accorded special attention: with these, indeed, she withdrew a moment to her own room. I softly rose in my bed and followed her with my eye: these keys, reader, were not brought back till they had left on the toilet of the adjoining room the impress of their wards in wax. All being thus done decently and in order, my property was returned to its place, my clothes were carefully refolded. Of what nature were the conclusions deduced from this scrutiny? Were they favourable or otherwise? Vain question. Madame's face of stone (for of stone in its present night-aspect it looked: it had been human and, as I said before, motherly, in the salon) betrayed no response.

Her duty done – I felt that in her eyes this business

was a duty – she rose, noiseless as a shadow: she moved towards her own chamber; at the door she turned, fixing her eye on the heroine of the bottle, who still slept and loudly snored. Mrs Svini (I presume this was Mrs Svini, Anglicé or Hibernice, Sweeny) – Mrs Sweeny's doom was in Madame Beck's eye – an immutable purpose that eye spoke: madame's visitations for shortcomings might be slow, but they were sure. All this was very un-English: truly I was in a foreign land.

The morrow made me further acquainted with Mrs Sweeny. It seems she had introduced herself to her present employer as an English lady in reduced circumstances: a native, indeed, of Middlesex, professing to speak the English tongue with the purest metropolitan accent. Madame – reliant on her own infallible expedients for finding out the truth in time – had a singular intrepidity in hiring service off-hand (as indeed seemed abundantly proved in my own case). She received Mrs Sweeny as nursery-governess to her three children. I need hardly explain to the reader that this lady was in effect a native of Ireland; her station I do not pretend to fix: she boldly declared that she had 'had the bringing-up of the son and daughter of a marquis.' I think, myself, she might possibly have been hanger-on, nurse, fosterer, or washerwoman, in some Irish family: she spoke a smothered brogue, curiously overlaid with mincing cockney inflections.

By some means or other she had acquired, and now held in possession, a wardrobe of rather suspicious splendour – gowns of stiff and costly silk, fitting her indifferently and apparently made for other proportions than those they now adorned; caps with real lace borders, and – the chief item in the inventory, the spell by which she struck a certain awe through the household, quelling the otherwise scornfully disposed teachers and servants, and, so long as her broad shoulders *wore* the folds of that majestic drapery, even influencing madame herself – *a real Indian shawl* – 'un véritable Cachmire,' as Madame Beck said, with mixed reverence and amaze. I feel quite sure that without this 'Cachmire' she would not have kept her footing in the pensionnat for two days: by virtue of it, and it only, she maintained the same a month.

But when Mrs Sweeny knew that I was come to fill her shoes, then it was that she declared herself – then did she rise on Madame Beck in her full power – then come down on me with her concentrated weight. Madame bore this revelation and visitation so well, so stoically, that I for very shame could not support it otherwise than with composure. For one little moment Madame Beck absented herself from the room; ten minutes after, an agent of the police stood in the midst of us. Mrs Sweeny and her effects were removed. Madame's brow had not been ruffled during the scene – her lips had not dropped one sharply accented word.

This brisk little affair of the dismissal was all set-tled before breakfast: order to march given, policeman called, mutineer expelled, 'chambre d'enfants' fumi-gated and cleansed, windows thrown open, and every trace of the accomplished Mrs Sweeny – even to the fine essence and spiritual fragrance which gave token so subtle and so fatal of the head and front of her offending – was annihilated from the Rue Fossette: all this, I say, was done between the moment of Madame Beck's issuing like Aurora from her chamber, and that in which she coolly sat down to pour out her first cup of coffee.

About noon, I was summoned to dress madame. (It appeared my place was to be a hybrid between gouvernante and lady's-maid). Till noon, she haunted the house in her wrapping-gown, shawl, and sound-less slippers. How would the lady-chief of an English school approve this custom?

The dressing of her hair puzzled me; she had plenty of it; auburn, unmixed with grey: though she was forty years old. Seeing my embarrassment, she said, 'You have not been a femme de chambre in your own country?' And taking the brush from my hand and setting me aside, not ungently or disre-spectfully, she arranged it herself. In performing other offices of the toilet, she half-directed, half-aided me, without the least display of temper or impatience. N.B. that was the first and last time I was required to dress her. Henceforth, on Rosine, the portress, devolved that duty.

When attired, Madame Beck appeared a personage of a figure rather short and stout, yet still graceful in its own peculiar way: that is, with the grace resulting from proportion of parts. Her complexion was fresh and sanguine, not too rubicund; her eye, blue and serene; her dark silk dress fitted her as a French sempstress alone can make a dress fit; she looked well, though a little bourgeoise: as bourgeoise, indeed, she was. I know not what of harmony pervaded her whole person; and yet her face offered contrast, too: its features were by no means such as are usually seen in conjunction with a complexion of such blended freshness and repose: their outline was stern; her forehead was high but narrow; it expressed capacity and some benevolence, but no expanse; nor did her peaceful yet watchful eye ever know the fire which is kindled in the heart or the softness which flows thence. Her mouth was hard: it could be a little grim; her lips were thin. For sensibility and genius, with all their tenderness and temerity, I felt somehow that madame would be the right sort of Minos in petticoats.

In the long run, I found that she was something else in petticoats too. Her name was Modeste Maria Beck, née Kint: it ought to have been Ignacia. She was a charitable woman, and did a great deal of good. There never was a mistress whose rule was milder. I was told that she never once remonstrated with the intolerable Mrs Sweeny, despite her tipsiness, disorder, and general neglect; yet Mrs Sweeny had to go, the moment her departure became convenient. I was told, too, that neither masters nor teachers were found fault with in that establishment; yet both masters and teachers were often changed: they vanished and others filled their places, none could well explain how.

The establishment was both a pensionnat and an externat: the externes or day-pupils exceeded one hundred in number; the boarders were about a score. Madame must have possessed high administrative powers: she ruled all these, together with four teachers, eight masters, six servants, and three children, managing at the same time to perfection the pupil's parents and friends; and that without apparent effort; without bustle, fatigue, fever, or any symptom of undue excitement: occupied she always was – busy, rarely. It is true that madame had her own system for managing and regulating this mass of machinery; and a very pretty system it was: the reader has seen a specimen of it, in that small affair of turning my pocket inside out, and reading my private memoranda. 'Surveillance,' 'espionage,' – these were her watch-words.

Still, madame knew what honesty was, and liked it – that is, when it did not obtrude its clumsy scruples in the way of her will and interest. She had a respect for 'Angleterre'; and as to 'les Anglaises,' she would have the women of no other country about her own children, if she could help it.

Often in the evening, after she had been plotting and counter-plotting, spying and receiving the reports of spies all day, she would come up to my room – a trace of real weariness on her brow – and she would sit down and listen while the children said their little prayers to me in English: the Lord's Prayer, and the hymn beginning 'Gentle Jesus,' these little Catholics were permitted to repeat at my knee; and, when I had put them to bed, she would talk to me (I soon gained enough French to be able to understand, and even answer her) about England and Englishwomen, and the reasons for what she was pleased to term their superior intelligence, and more real and reliable probity. Very good sense she often showed; very sound opinions she often broached: she seemed to know that keeping girls in distrustful restraint, in blind ignorance, and under a surveillance that left them no moment and no corner for retirement, was not the best way to make them grow up honest and modest women; but she averred that ruinous consequences would ensue if any other method were tried with continental children – they were so accustomed to constraint, that relaxation, however guarded, would be misunderstood and fatally presumed on: she was sick, she would declare, of the means she had to use, but use them she must; and after discoursing, often with dignity and delicacy to me, she would move away on her 'souliers de silence,' and glide ghostlike through the house watching and spying everywhere, peering through every key-hole, listening behind every door.

After all, madame's system was not bad – let me do her justice. Nothing could be better than all her arrangements for the physical well-being of her scholars. No minds were overtasked; the lessons were well distributed and made incomparably easy to the learner; there was a liberty of amusement, and a provision for exercise which kept the girls healthy; the food was abundant and good: neither pale nor puny faces were anywhere to be seen in the Rue Fossette. She never grudged a holiday; she allowed plenty of time for sleeping, dressing, washing, eating; her method in all these matters was easy, liberal, salutary, and rational: many an austere English school-mistress would do vastly well to imitate it – and I believe many would be glad to do so, if exacting English parents would let them.

As Madame Beck ruled by espionage, she of course had her staff of spies: she perfectly knew the quality of the tools she used, and while she would not scruple to handle the dirtiest for a dirty occasion – flinging this sort from her like refuse rind, after the orange has been duly squeezed – I have known her fastidious in seeking pure metal for clean uses; and when once a bloodless and rustless instrument was found, she was careful of the prize, keeping it in silk and cotton-wool. Yet, woe be to that man or woman who relied on her one inch beyond the point where it was her interest to be trustworthy: interest was the master-key of madame's nature – the mainspring of her motives – the alpha and omega of her life. I have seen her *feelings* appealed to, and I have smiled in half-pity, half-scorn at the appellants. None ever gained her ear through that channel, or swayed her purpose by that means. On the contrary, to attempt to touch her heart was the surest way to rouse her antipathy, and to make of her a secret foe. It proved to her that she had no heart to be touched: it reminded her where she was impotent and dead. Never was the distinction between charity and mercy better exemplified than in her. While devoid of sympathy, she had a sufficiency of rational benevolence: she would give in the readiest manner to people she had never seen – rather, however, to classes than to individuals. 'Pour les pauvres,' she opened her purse freely – against *the poor man*, as a rule, she kept it closed. In philanthropic schemes, for the benefit of society at large, she took a cheerful part; no private sorrow touched her: no force or mass of suffering concentrated in one heart had power to pierce hers. Not the agony in

Gethsemane, not the death on Calvary, could have wrung from her eyes one tear.

I say again, madame was a very great and a very capable woman. That school offered for her powers too limited a sphere; she ought to have swayed a nation: she should have been the leader of a turbulent legislative assembly. Nobody could have brow-beaten her, none irritated her nerves, exhausted her patience, or overreached her astuteness. In her own single person, she could have comprised the duties of a first minister and a superintendent of police. Wise, firm, faithless; secret, crafty, passionless; watchful and inscrutable; acute and insensate – withal perfectly decorous – what more could be desired?

The sensible reader will not suppose that I gained all the knowledge here condensed for his benefit in one month, or in one half-year. No! what I saw at first was the thriving outside of a large and flourishing educational establishment. Here was a great house, full of healthy, lively girls, all well-dressed and many of them handsome, gaining knowledge by a marvellously easy method, without painful exertion or useless waste of spirits; not, perhaps, making very rapid progress in anything; taking it easy, but still always employed, and never oppressed. Here was a corps of teachers and masters more stringently tasked, as all the real head-labour was to be done by them, in order to save the pupils, yet having their duties so arranged that they relieved each other in quick succession whenever the work was severe; here, in short, was a foreign school; of which the life, movement, and variety made it a complete and most charming contrast to many English institutions of the same kind.

Behind the house was a large garden, and, in summer, the pupils almost lived out of doors amongst the rose-bushes and the fruit-trees. Under the vast and vine-draped berceau, madame would take her seat on summer afternoons, and send for the classes, in turns, to sit round her and sew and read. Meantime, masters came and went, delivering short and lively lectures, rather than lessons, and the pupils made notes of their instructions, or did *not* make them – just as inclination prompted; secure that, in case of neglect, they could copy the notes of their companions. Besides the regular monthly *jours de sortie*, the Catholic fête-days brought a succession of holidays all the year round; and sometimes on a bright summer morning, or soft summer evening, the boarders were taken out for a long walk into the country, regaled with *gaufres* and *vin blanc*, or new milk and *pain bis*, or *pistolets au beurre* (rolls) and coffee. All this seemed very pleasant, and madame appeared goodness itself; and the teachers not so bad, but they might be worse; and the pupils, perhaps, a little noisy and rough, but types of health and glee.

Thus did the view appear, seen through the enchantment of distance; but there came a time when distance was to melt for me, when I was to be called down from my watch-tower of the nursery, whence I had hitherto made my observations, and was to be compelled into closer intercourse with this little world of the Rue Fossette.

I was one day sitting up-stairs, as usual, hearing the children their English lessons, and at the same time turning a silk dress for madame, when she came sauntering into the room with that absorbed air and brow of hard thought she sometimes wore, and which made her look so little genial. Dropping into a seat opposite mine, she remained some minutes silent. Désirée, the eldest girl, was reading to me some little essay of Mrs Barbauld's, and I was making her translate currently from English to French as she proceeded, by way of ascertaining that she comprehended what she read: madame listened.

Presently, without preface or prelude, she said, almost in the tone of one making an accusation, 'Meess, in England you were a governess.'

'No, madame,' said I smiling, 'you are mistaken.'

'Is this your first essay at teaching – this attempt with my children?'

I assured her it was. Again she became silent; but looking up, as I took a pin from the cushion, I found myself an object of study: she held me under her eye;

she seemed turning me round in her thoughts – measuring my fitness for a purpose, weighing my value in a plan. Madame had, ere this, scrutinized all I had, and I believe she esteemed herself cognizant of much that I was; but from that day, for the space of about a fortnight, she tried me by new tests. She listened at the nursery door when I was shut in with the children; she followed me at a cautious distance when I walked out with them, stealing within earshot whenever the trees of park or boulevard afforded a sufficient screen: a strict preliminary process having thus been observed, she made a move forward.

One morning, coming on me abruptly, and with the semblance of hurry, she said she found herself placed in a little dilemma. Mr Wilson, the English master, had failed to come at his hour, she feared he was ill; the pupils were waiting in classe; there was no one to give a lesson; should I, for once, object to giving a short dictation exercise, just that the pupils might not have it to say they had missed their English lesson?

'In classe, madam?' I asked.

'Yes, in classe: in the second division.'

'Where there are sixty pupils,' said I; for I knew the number, and with my usual base habit of cowardice, I shrunk into my sloth, like a snail into its shell, and alleged incapacity and impracticability as a pretext to escape action. If left to myself, I should infallibly have let this chance slip. Inadventurous, unstirred by impulses of practical ambition, I was capable of sitting twenty years teaching infants the hornbook, turning silk dresses, and making children's frocks. Not that true contentment dignified this infatuated resignation: my work had neither charm for my taste, nor hold on my interest; but it seemed to me a great thing to be without heavy anxiety, and relieved from intimate trial; the negation of severe suffering was the nearest approach to happiness I expected to know. Besides, I seemed to hold two lives – the life of thought, and that of reality; and, provided the former was nourished with a sufficiency of the strange necromantic joys of fancy, the privileges of the latter might remain limited to daily bread, hourly work, and a roof of shelter.

'Come,' said madame, as I stooped more busily than ever over the cutting out of a child's pinafore, 'leave that work.'

'But Fifine wants it, madame.'

'Fifine must want it, then, for I want *you*.'

And as Madame Beck did really want and was resolved to have me – as she had long been dissatisfied with the English master, with his short-comings in punctuality, and his careless method of tuition – as, too, *she* did not lack resolution and practical activity, whether *I* lacked them or not – she, without more ado, made me relinquish thimble and needle;

my hand was taken into hers, and I was conducted down stairs. When we reached the carré, a large square hall between the dwelling-house and the pensionnat, she paused, dropped my hand, faced, and scrutinized me. I was flushed, and tremulous from head to foot; tell it not in Gath, I believe I was crying. In fact, the difficulties before me were far from being wholly imaginary; some of them were real enough; and not the least substantial lay in my want of mastery over the medium through which I should be obliged to teach. I had, indeed, studied French closely since my arrival in Villette; learning its practice by day, and its theory in every leisure moment at night, to as late an hour as the rule of the house would allow candle-light, but I was far from yet being able to trust my powers of correct oral expression.

'Dites donc,' said madame sternly, 'vous sentez vous réellement trop faible?'

I might have said 'Yes,' and gone back to nursery obscurity, and there, perhaps, mouldered for the rest of my life; but, looking up at madame, I saw in her countenance a something that made me think twice ere I decided. At that instant, she did not wear a woman's aspect, but rather a man's. Power of a particular kind strongly limned itself in all her traits, and that power was not *my* kind of power: neither sympathy, nor congeniality, nor submission, were the emotions it awakened. I stood – not soothed, nor won, nor overwhelmed. It seemed as if a challenge of strength between opposing gifts was given, and I suddenly felt all the dishonour of my diffidence – all the pusillanimity of my slackness to aspire.

'Will you,' said she, 'go backward or forward?' indicating with her hand, first, the small door of communication with the dwelling-house, and then the great double portals of the classes or schoolrooms.

'En avant,' I said.

'But,' pursued she, cooling as I warmed, and continuing the hard look, from very antipathy to which I drew strength and determination, 'can you face the classes, or are you over-excited?'

She sneered slightly in saying this – nervous excitability was not much to madame's taste.

'I am no more excited than this stone,' I said, tapping the flag with my toe: 'or than you,' I added, returning her look.

'Bon! But let me tell you these are not quiet, decorous English girls you are going to encounter. Ce sont des Labassecouriennes, rondes, franches, brusques, et tant soit peu rebelles.'

I said: 'I know; and I know, too, that though I have studied French hard since I came here yet I still speak it with far too much hesitation – too little accuracy to be able to command their respect: I shall make blunders that will lay me open to the scorn of the most ignorant. Still I mean to give the lesson.'

'They always throw over timid teachers,' said she.

'I know that, too, madame; I have heard how they rebelled against and persecuted Miss Turner' – a poor, friendless English teacher, whom madame had employed, and lightly discarded; and to whose piteous history I was no stranger.

'C'est vrai,' said she, coolly. 'Miss Turner had no more command over them than a servant from the kitchen would have had. She was weak and wavering; she had neither tact nor intelligence, decision nor dignity. Miss Turner would not do for these girls at all.'

I made no reply, but advanced to the closed schoolroom door.

'You will not expect aid from me, or from any one,' said madame. 'That would at once set you down as incompetent for your office.'

I opened the door, let her pass with courtesy, and followed her. There were three school-rooms, all large. That dedicated to the second division, where I was to figure, was considerably the largest, and accommodated an assemblage more numerous, more turbulent, and infinitely more unmanageable than the other two. In after days, when I knew the ground better, I used to think sometimes (if such a comparison may be permitted), that the quiet, polished, tame first division, was to the robust, riotous demonstrative second division, what the English House of Lords is to the House of Commons.

The first glance informed me that many of the pupils were more than girls – quite young women; I knew that some of them were of noble family (as nobility goes in Labassecour), and I was well convinced that not one amongst them was ignorant of my position in madame's household. As I mounted the estrade (a low platform, raised a step above the flooring), where stood the teacher's chair and desk, I beheld opposite to me a row of eyes and brows that threatened stormy weather – eyes full of an insolent light, and brows hard and unblushing as marble. The continental 'female' is quite a different being to the insular 'female' of the same age and class: I never saw such eyes and brows in England. Madame Beck introduced me in one cool phrase, sailed from the room, and left me alone in my glory.

I shall never forget that first lesson, nor all the undercurrent of life and character it opened up to me. Then first did I begin rightly to see the wide difference that lies between the novelist's and poet's ideal 'jeune fille,' and the said 'jeune fille' as she really is.

It seems that three titled belles in the first row had sat down predetermined that a *bonne d'enfants* should not give them lessons in English. They knew they had succeeded in expelling obnoxious teachers before now; they knew that madame would at any time throw overboard a professeur or maîtresse who became unpopular with the school – that she never assisted a weak official to retain his place – that if he had not strength to fight, or tact to win his way – down he went: looking at 'Miss Snowe' they promised themselves an easy victory.

Mesdemoiselles Blanche, Virginie, and Angélique opened the campaign by a series of titterings and whisperings; these soon swelled into murmurs and short laughs, which the remoter benches caught up and echoed more loudly. This growing revolt of sixty against one, soon became oppressive enough; my command of French being so limited, and exercised under such cruel constraint.

Could I but have spoken in my own tongue, I felt as if I might have gained a hearing; for, in the first place, though I knew I looked a poor creature, and in many respects actually was so, yet nature had given me a voice that could make itself heard, if lifted in excitement or deepened by emotion. In the second place, while I had no flow, only a hesitating trickle of language, in ordinary circumstances, yet – under stimulus such as was now rife through the mutinous mass – I could, in English, have rolled out readily phrases stigmatizing their proceedings as such proceedings deserved to be stigmatized; and then with some sarcasm, flavoured with contemptuous bitterness, for the ringleaders, and relieved with easy banter for the weaker, but less knavish followers, it seemed to me that one might possibly get command over this wild herd and bring them into training, at least. All I could now do was to walk up to Blanche – Mademoiselle de Melcy, a young baronne – the eldest, tallest, handsomest, and most vicious – stand before her desk, take from under her hand her exercise-book, remount the estrade, deliberately read the composition, which I found very stupid, and as deliberately, and in the face of the whole school, tear the blotted page in two.

This action availed to draw attention and check noise. One girl alone, quite in the background, persevered in the riot with undiminished energy. I looked at her attentively. She had a pale face, hair like night, broad strong eyebrows, decided features, and a dark, mutinous, sinister eye: I noted that she sat close by a little door, which door, I was well aware, opened into a small closet where books were kept. She was standing up for the purpose of conducting her clamour with freer energies. I measured her stature and calculated her strength. She seemed both tall and wiry; but, so the conflict were brief and the attack unexpected, I thought I might manage her.

Advancing up the room, looking as cool and careless as I possibly could, in short, *ayant l'air de rien*; I slightly pushed the door and found it was ajar. In an instant, and with sharpness, I had turned on her. In another instant she occupied the closet, the door was shut, and the key in my pocket.

It so happened that this girl, Dolores by name and a Catalonian by race, was the sort of character at once dreaded and hated by all her associates; the act of summary justice above noted, proved popular: there was not one present but, in her heart, liked to see it done. They were stilled for a moment; then a smile – not a laugh – passed from desk to desk: then – when I had gravely and tranquilly returned to the estrade, courteously requested silence, and commenced a dictation as if nothing at all had happened – the pens travelled peacefully over the pages, and the remainder of the lesson passed in order and industry.

'C'est bien,' said Madame Beck, when I came out of class, hot and a little exhausted. 'Ça ira.'

She had been listening and peeping through a spy-hole the whole time.

From that day I ceased to be nursery-governess, and became English teacher. Madame raised my salary; but she got thrice the work out of me she had extracted from Mr Wilson, at half the expense.

． ． ．

PAULINA MARY SOUGHT my frequent presence in the Rue Crécy. In the old Bretton days, though she had never professed herself fond of me, my society had soon become to her a sort of unconscious necessary. I used to notice that if I withdrew to my room, she would speedily come trotting after me, and opening the door and peeping in, say, with her little peremptory accent, –

'Come down. Why do you sit here by yourself? You must come into the parlour.'

In the same spirit she urged me now –

'Leave the Rue Fossette,' she said, 'and come and live with us. Papa would give you far more than Madame Beck gives you.'

Mr Home himself offered me a handsome sum – thrice my present salary – if I would accept the office of companion to his daughter. I declined. I think I should have declined had I been poorer than I was, and with scantier fund of resource, more stinted narrowness of future prospect. I had not that vocation. I could teach; I could give lessons; but to be either a private governess or a companion was unnatural to me. Rather than fill the former post in any great house, I would deliberately have taken a housemaid's place, bought a strong pair of gloves, swept bedrooms and staircases, and cleaned stoves and locks, in peace and independence. Rather than be a companion, I would have made shirts, and starved.

I was no bright lady's shadow – not Miss de Bassompierre's. Overcast enough it was my nature often to be; of a subdued habit I was: but the dimness and depression must both be voluntary – such as kept me docile at my desk, in the midst of my now well-accustomed pupils in Madame Beck's first classe; or alone, at my own bedside, in her dormitory, or in the alley and seat which were called mine, in her garden: my qualifications were not convertible, not adaptable; they could not be made the foil of any gem, and adjunct of any beauty, the appendage of any greatness in Christendom. Madame Beck and I, without assimilating, understood each other well. I was not *her* companion, nor her children's governess; she left me free: she tied me to nothing – not to herself – not even to her interests: once, when she had for a fortnight been called from home by a near relation's illness, and on her return, all anxious and full of care about her establishment, lest something in her absence should have gone wrong – finding that matters had proceeded much as usual, and that there was no evidence of glaring neglect – she made each of the teachers a present, in acknowledgement of steadiness. To my bedside she came at twelve o'clock at night, and told me she had no present for me. 'I must make fidelity advantageous to the St Pierre,' said she; 'if I attempt to make it advantageous to you, there will arise misunderstanding between us – perhaps separation. One thing, however, I *can* do to please you – leave you alone with your liberty: c'est ce que je ferai.'

She kept her word. Every slight shackle she had ever laid on me, she, from that time, with quiet hand removed. Thus I had pleasure in voluntarily respecting her rules; gratification in devoting double time, in taking double pains with the pupils she committed to my charge.

. . .

'LIVING COSTS LITTLE,' said I to myself, 'in this economical town of Villette, where people are more sensible than I understand they are in dear old England – infinitely less worried about appearance, and less emulous of display – where nobody is in the least ashamed to be quite as homely and saving as he finds convenient. House-rent, in a prudently chosen situation, need not be high. When I shall have saved one thousand francs, I will take a tenement with one large room, and two or three smaller ones, furnish the first with a few benches and desks, a black tableau, an estrade for myself; upon it a chair and table, with a sponge and some white chalks; begin with taking day-pupils, and so work my way upwards. Madame Beck's commencement was – as I have often heard her say – from no higher starting-point, and where is she now? All these premises and this garden are hers, bought with her money; she has a competency already secured for old age, and a flourishing establishment under her direction, which will furnish a career for her children.

Courage, Lucy Snowe! With self-denial and economy now, and steady exertion by-and-by, an object in life need not fail you. Venture not to complain that such an object is too selfish, too limited, and lacks interest; be content to labour for independence until you have proved, by winning that prize, your right to look higher.

CHARLOTTE BRONTË was born on 21 April 1816. Her father was curate of Haworth, Yorkshire and her mother died when she was just five years old. In 1824 Charlotte and her sisters Maria, Elizabeth and Emily were sent to a school for clergymen's daughters, where Maria and Elizabeth both caught tuberculosis and died. The remaining children were taught at home from this point on and together they created vivid fantasy worlds which they explored by writing stories. Charlotte worked as a teacher and then as a governess but in 1847 *Jane Eyre* was published to immediate success. Between 1848 and 1849 Charlotte lost her remaining siblings: Emily, Branwell and Anne. She died on 31 March 1855.

RECOMMENDED BOOKS BY CHARLOTTE BRONTË:

Jane Eyre
Villette
Shirley

JANE EYRE

As an orphan, Jane's childhood is not an easy one but her independence and strength of character keep her going through the miseries inflicted by cruel relatives and a brutal school. However, her biggest challenge is yet to come. Taking a job as a governess in a house full of secrets, for a passionate man she grows more and more attracted to, ultimately forces Jane to call on all her resources in order to hold on to her beliefs.

Jane Eyre is the inspiring heroine of one of the best-loved British novels of all time.

'After all these years, it's the emotions we most respond to in Jane Eyre . . . This is also a novel about intellectual growth, written by a fiercely intelligent writer . . . She has a formidable brain as well as a strongly beating heart, and so it will still seem another 100 years from now' *Guardian*

'One of the most perfectly structured novels of all time' *Sarah Waters*

'At the end we are steeped through and through with the genius, the vehemence, the indignation of Charlotte Brontë' *Virginia Woolf*

VINTAGE MINIS

The Vintage Minis bring you the world's greatest writers on the experiences that make us human. These stylish, entertaining little books explore the whole spectrum of life – from birth to death, and everything in between. Which means there's something here for everyone, whatever your story.

vintageminis.co.uk